Naomi's Song

NAOMI'S SONG

Selma Kritzer Silverberg

2009 • 5769
Philadelphia

JPS is a nonprofit educational association and the oldest and foremost publisher of Judaica in English in North America. The mission of JPS is to enhance Jewish culture by promoting the dissemination of religious and secular works, in the United States and abroad, to all individuals and institutions interested in past and contemporary Jewish life.

The Jewish Publication Society
2100 Arch Street, 2nd floor
Philadelphia, PA 19103
www.jewishpub.org

Design and Composition by Claudia Capelli
Cover illustration and design by Avi Katz

Manufactured in the United States of America

09 10 11 12   10 9 8 7 6 5 4 3 2 1

Library of Congress Cataloging-in-Publication Data:

Silverberg, Selma Kritzer

Naomi's song / Selma Silverberg.— 1st ed.
    p. cm.
    Summary: Elaborates on the biblical story of Naomi, who grows up and marries in twelfth century B.C. Judaea, moves with her husband and sons to Moab, and returns home with her daughter-in-law Ruth, facing many trials with faith and perseverance.
    ISBN 978-0-8276-0886-3 (alk. paper)
    1. Naomi (Biblical figure)—Juvenile fiction 2. Ruth (Biblical figure)—Juvenile fiction. [1. Naomi (Biblical figure)—Fiction 2. Ruth (Biblical figure)—Fiction. 3. Women—History—To 1500—Fiction. 4. Jews—History—1200-953 B.C.—Fiction. 5. Judaea (Region)—Fiction. 6. Moab (Kingdom)—Fiction.] I. Title.
    PZ7.S58582Nao 2009

    [Fic]—-dc22

                        2008034888

JPS books are available at discounts for bulk purchases for reading groups, special sales, and fundraising purchases. Custom editions, including personalized covers, can be created in larger quantities for special needs. For more information, please contact us at marketing@jewishpub.org or at this address: 2100 Arch Street, Philadelphia, PA 19103.

I dedicate this book to my beloved children and grandchildren—

my kinderleben.

S.K.S.

FOREWORD

The Hidden Manuscript of *Naomi's Song*

Naomi's Song was written by Selma Kritzer Silverberg in the 1950s, but it lay hidden until it was discovered in the spring of 2005. Selma Silverberg was my mother. The recovery of this manuscript as my mother was dying echoes the theme of *Naomi's Song*, a story of self-discovery and the strength of women. Its hiddenness parallels a lifetime in which my mother, like so many women born in the first decade of the twentieth century, hid her voice and quietly chose among a limited set of options within the cultural norms of her generation.

Mother had written *Naomi's Song* with the intention of presenting it to me for my sixteenth birthday in 1959, but it took her nine more years to complete it. In the 1960s there was not a big market for biblical fiction for teenage girls and she could not find a publisher, so it lay on her bookshelf, untouched.

In 1984 she made photocopies of the hand-typed manuscript for each of her five granddaughters and wrote a preface, ending with these sentences: "Naomi was a female of little note in ancient Israel. Hence, to win a place for herself, she evolved necessary convictions and courage—qualities I wish for my five beautiful granddaughters."

The manuscript was not thought of again for twenty years, until Mother's curious hospice aide discovered it on her shelf, read it, and enthused about it to me. At that point I reread it and was struck by the relevancy of the biblical story and the quality of the research and writing. Mother died at the age of ninety-six in April 2005, twenty-one years after she wrote the dedication and almost forty years after her original draft of the book.

What followed in bringing this book to life Mother would have credited to God's handiwork. She was a profoundly committed Jew and enjoyed a personal relationship with God that sustained her during her entire life. She always talked things over with God, prayed to God when she needed help, and gave thanks to her "Gracious Lord" at every opportunity.

After her death the family observed the traditional one-week mourning period. Many friends came to support us in our loss. We reminisced about her and took the opportunity to share the joy of knowing her with them. We talked about her love of writing, and how she had self-published a children's book about the Shaker people who lived in Cleveland in the mid-1800s. That booklet was later reprinted and distributed by the Shaker Historical Museum.

I also mentioned the unpublished manuscript of *Naomi's Song*, and one night after everyone else had left, our friend Rabbi Jeffrey Schein, a Jewish educator, asked if he could read it. His response was very positive, and at his suggestion I submitted the manuscript to the Jewish Publication Society (JPS). To me, as if by divine intervention, JPS offered to publish the book.

Throughout this process of discovery I realized that I had little knowledge of the dynamic, talented, and accomplished part of my mother's persona. She was a seemingly conventional woman of her times: a "good wife and mother" and an active volunteer for good causes. She always put others first to let their lights shine. She was an excellent listener with a knack for focusing on and remembering what was important to each person.

But there were clues to the empowered woman who lay beneath this conventional facade. She was quietly determined and persevering. Born a natural teacher, she did not start college until the age of forty-four, taking only one course per semester to avoid disrupting family life, and graduated fourteen years later. During her "housewife" years she not only wrote the aforementioned books and other articles, but also compiled a history of Yiddish music, which she presented in senior citizen venues. She was always studying and had a broad range of interests: the Bible, bridge, Spanish, Hebrew, and in later years politics.

Her elaborate and joyous celebrations of Shabbat and the Jewish holidays were her hallmark. She had such confidence, creativity, and joy in her Judaism that she inspired and stimulated others to emulate her—or at least to open their hearts and minds to what Judaism has to offer. For years she also volunteered as a Sunday school teacher.

Putting the clues together, I rediscovered my mother as a powerful force who affected many lives, but in her own immediate family her voice was secondary to her husband's. This was her choice—a "good" wife needed to put her husband in the limelight while she remained in the background. Her voice should not be too strong. This message was passed along to me, her only daughter.

Just as in her dedication, and just as in ancient Israel, women's voices were of "little note"—so women need to develop, then and now, "necessary convictions and courage." Mother's convictions came through clearly in many ways: her creative home celebrations; her tradition of a nightly bedtime Jewish prayer; her advocacy of positive thinking; and her volunteerism.

In later years she wrote monthly letters to her children, whom she called her "kinderleben" (beloved children). Relatives and close friends heard about these letters and asked to be included in the "kinderleben" mailings until she was photocopying and mailing close to fifty letters a month. In these letters she had free rein to teach, moralize, address injustices, and detail her many current interests. She shared with us her convictions, her courage, and her curiosity. She urged us to go into politics to shape the world around us. Always, her compassion and understanding shone through, and all of us felt enlightened and inspired by her teachings and writings.

The publication of *Naomi's Song* brings to fruition her lifelong goals of teaching, Bible storytelling, and empowering girls to have that "necessary conviction and courage." For me, the discovery of her manuscript opened a vista to the fully empowered woman that she quietly was—and that she wrote about in *Naomi's Song*.

—Judy Vida (nee Silverberg)

PREFACE

I wrote *Naomi's Song* as a gift for my daughter, Judy, on her sixteenth birthday, September 7, 1959.

Now, in April 1984, it is appropriate that I present *Naomi's Song* to you at this season, since my story is based on the biblical Book of Ruth, which is customarily read in synagogues during the springtime festival of Shavuot.

Naomi was a female of little note in ancient Israel. Hence, to win a place for herself, she evolved necessary convictions and courage—qualities I wish for my five beautiful granddaughters: Susan, Lisa, Gwen, Jo Hana, and Maryn.

Lovingly,

Savtah

ACKNOWLEDGMENTS

My heartfelt thanks go to the following "angels" who offered their support, guidance, and expertise to bring *Naomi's Song* to life: Suzy Whelan; Rabbi Jeffrey Schein; Kathy Wisch; Bea Silverberg; Anna Kelman; Rachel Lerner; Jeff Marks; Seth Marks; Brian Miller; Barry Epstein; Deedee Paster; Rena Potok and Janet Liss of The Jewish Publication Society; Rose Wayne; my husband, Peter Gray; and my brothers and my sisters-in-law, Ted, Natalie, Dan, and Linda Silverberg.

Finally, in my mother's words, I give thanks to the "Gracious Lord."

—Judy Vida (nee Silverberg)

Editor's Note

"Judeans" was the name given to Jews (known at the time as Hebrews) and others who lived in the kingdom of Judea during the time of Naomi and Ruth.

Book I

Naomi
and
Elimelek

"Naomi, run! Warn the city!"

From the distance of the wheat field, the ten-year-old girl heard her mother's terror-stricken scream. With a start, she dropped the sheaf of wheat she was binding and turned toward her family's farm yard. It was full of soldiers, tall, strong, dangerous soldiers. Panic welled up in Naomi's throat. *Where were her parents, her uncle,* she wondered. There! In the center of the soldiers stood her father and her uncle. The soldiers beat them, landing blow after blow with their fists and their knives. The two men stumbled and did not get up. The soldiers who had been restraining Naomi's weeping mother led her away.

Heart pounding, Naomi screamed to her aunt Tirza, "Auntie, come! Please!" She ran over and forced the frightened woman's fingers from her bundle. Naomi and her aunt ran through the fields to the fortified city of Bethlehem as the soldiers shot arrows that whizzed past their heads.

The watchmen in the towers sounded the alarms. "Faster! Come faster!" they called. The men in the marketplace strained to close the heavy wooden gates. A moment after Naomi and Tirza ran in, the huge doors slammed shut and the Judean men scrambled up to guard the walls.

These were the years when the Judeans of Bethlehem, with no king or army to protect them, suffered frequent surprise attacks by their neighbors. Only a few generations before, the Judeans, and all the Israelites, had been slaves in Egypt under Pharaoh. Now they ruled themselves with a Council of Elders, but constant vigilance or death was the price they paid for their freedom.

"Where will we go?" Tirza asked.

"Perhaps Uncle Hepher will take us in," Naomi suggested.

Hepher was the eldest brother to Naomi's father and to Tirza's husband. He and his family were almost like strangers, but where else was there to go?

When Naomi and Tirza arrived at Hepher's house, he made no attempt to hide his displeasure. "I don't need two more women in my home." Then he told a servant to take his niece and his sister-in-law to the women's quarters. "Give them the food for mourners, bread and water."

And there, for seven days, the frail widow and orphan huddled in a corner. They wept until their eyes swelled. Hepher had two wives and many sons and daughters, but not one of them spoke to Naomi and Tirza. Although weak from having eaten only the mourner's portion of bread and water, Naomi whispered to her aunt about their future.

"Auntie, do you think they will like us? What would Father and Mother say if they knew we were here? Auntie, I'll try to work hard for Uncle Hepher."

Tirza looked into her innocent niece's face and began to weep again. "I can only think of my husband, Machir," she whispered back.

On the day after the end of the seven days of mourning, Avishag, Hepher's eleven-year-old daughter, beckoned to Naomi. "Follow me. We need firewood."

The two girls joined the streams of people hurrying to the marketplace. It was difficult for the tall Naomi to look into the face of her short, pretty cousin, who was walking very fast, but Naomi said to her, "Avishag, will you be my friend? I mean, besides being my cousin?"

Avishag didn't answer, as she quickened her pace, elbowing into the throng that jostled its way from the marketplace out through the open gates of the city. At that early hour, the Judean workers were leaving the town: a solid mass of farmers, woodcutters, water-carriers, shepherds, vineyard-workers, tree-dressers, travelers, and children like Naomi and Avishag going out to gather firewood for the bake-ovens.

Naomi, breathlessly keeping up, persisted. "Will you, Avishag? Be my friend?"

The city girl was annoyed with her awkward farm cousin, who was as muscular and strong as a boy. "Why?" she asked.

"Because I've never had a friend of my own. On our farm in Ephrat, we had no neighbors with children my age."

"But why did you come to us?"

"Aunt Tirza and I have no other relatives."

Avishag shrugged. "Look, if we don't hurry with the firewood, the bread won't be baked. You gather brush on this side, and I'll go over there."

Naomi joined the other children in the task of gathering firewood. She was glad to be outdoors again, to stretch her body, cramped from a week's inactivity, and she was glad to see the familiar sight of streams, orchards, and fields filled with harvesters. She closed her mind to the pain in her heart. *In Sheol, the afterworld, Father and Mother will be proud of my behavior*, she said to herself.

She set to work uprooting the woody underbrush and pulling down the dry branches that the smaller children couldn't reach. She broke the branches into twigs and had a sizable pile in a short time. Just as she was picking up the pile in her arms, Avishag came up. "Here's my wood," she said as she dropped a bundle of sticks. "My friends are waiting. Take my wood home with yours."

She ran off before Naomi could say a word. The pile was too large now for her to carry alone, so she stood there, undecided, as Avishag's sisters and brothers' wives came along the path with their empty water jugs.

"You there, why are you idling?" scolded Eglah, the oldest. "Get home with the wood. You know the mothers are waiting."

Naomi scooped up the pile as best she could and returned to the city. When townspeople thoughtlessly bumped into her, the dry twigs, barbed and spiny, made her arms bleed.

What seemed like hours later, she reached the front yard where Hepher's two wives waited. His first wife, Hoglah, greeted her. "Is that all you brought? If you want bread today, you'll have to show more effort."

Twice more, Naomi went out of the city and returned with loaded arms, never once seeing Avishag. Weary after dragging home the last pile, she dropped it at the outdoor bake-oven.

The yard was noisy and overcrowded. Hepher's wives, daughters, daughters-in-law, and grandchildren worked, ate, and played there. Naomi waited for a friendly word. Michal, the second wife, said, "Don't stand there. Finish baking the bread."

Naomi's heart sank. All she knew of bread baking was what she saw when her mother threw the flat wheels of dough against the inside walls of the hot oven. She had never tried getting the bread out, but she didn't tell the two mothers. They would think her unwilling to work.

When Hoglah came by to gather the baked loaves, she stared at the young baker's hands, which were raw and blistered from having touched the hot oven walls. "Idiot!" she said. "You don't know anything about baking bread."

Humiliated, Naomi turned away. She saw her aunt on the far side of the yard. Tirza, who was too weak to use anything heavier than a mortar and pestle, kneeled and crushed grain.

Naomi ran to her aunt's side. "Auntie, I'll do it," she said as she pulled the stone roller from Tirza's hands. She knelt down, but before she could crush the roller down on the grain, someone pulled her up by the hair and slapped her across the face.

It was Hoglah, red with anger. "How dare you change my orders. Let the sloth do what I told her!"

Naomi gasped. She had never been slapped before.

That night, Naomi and Tirza sat with the women, waiting patiently while the men ate. When the men left, the women rose and called to the children. They all sat in the vacated seats. But no one invited Tirza and Naomi to the table. Naomi's stomach growled loudly, but she and her aunt could not presume to sit down to the meal unasked.

When the women and children had finished eating, Michal said on her way out, "You two do not deserve our husband's generosity. Clean the bowls."

Naomi ran to the table and searched through every bowl for scraps. She licked and sucked out all she could, careful to keep the few whole pieces for Tirza.

"Come here, Auntie. See what I'm saving for you. Aren't you as hungry as I am?"

But Tirza didn't move. She looked shrunken, her eyes hollow. Naomi asked again. "Why won't you eat?" And then she saw the tears on Tirza's face. "Auntie, what's wrong here? Why are we treated this way? Why don't you tell Uncle Hepher?"

Tirza answered in measured tones. "Hepher's family doesn't need me. They have many hands for every task. I have no place here."

"Surely you could marry and leave. You're so lovely."

Tirza shook her head. "Who would have me? The Law concerning widows says that Hepher must take me as a third wife so that I should beget sons to keep Machir's name and inheritance alive. But Hepher knows, as all Bethlehem knows, that I'm unable to give birth. Machir could have taken a second wife, but he loved me—only me—and didn't ask for sons."

Naomi lost her zest for the food. "There must be another way," she said.

"No, there's no other way for me. I'm too old to bond myself to a master for the food I eat because there's no hard work left in me. I'm too weak to hire out for field labor, and besides, that's only at harvest time. I would starve in the streets, Naomi, and I can't bring that shame on Machir."

Heavily, Tirza rose and went to the table, but not to eat. She wiped the empty bowls clean and as she turned them upside down in readiness for the next meal, she didn't have to face Naomi while she talked. Her voice weak with hopelessness, she said, "Forgive me, child, for saying this, but without my Machir I wish . . . I wish that my fate had been the same as your mother's, to be taken away and killed."

Naomi couldn't speak.

"If you love me, I ask you not to interfere with the work I'm told to do. The sooner my life comes to an end, the sooner my spirit can join Machir's in the land of Sheol."

Naomi ran to the women's bedroom, where she threw herself down on the rush mat and cried.

Sometime later, Eglah stood above her. "My father wants to see you."

Naomi wiped her eyes and followed Eglah to the outside stairway that led up to the flat rooftop, the cool porch of the house. Hepher sat there surrounded by his six sons, his two wives, his nine daughters, and his sons' wives. "Naomi," he said, "I have heard bad accounts of you today. Explain yourself."

Naomi didn't understand what her uncle meant.

"If you wish to live in harmony here, you cannot afford to be idle while the rest of us work. It has come to me that this morning, while Avishag went far afield to gather fuel, you picked up her bundles and claimed them as your work. She was worn out with her efforts and came home crying and empty-handed."

Naomi couldn't believe her ears. "That's not true," she protested. "I picked all the wood and carried it home. Only once did Avishag ask me to carry hers with mine. The rest I did alone, twice more!"

She turned to her cousin. "Avishag, tell them the truth."

Avishag looked away, then burst into tears and threw herself into her father's arms.

Michal pointed a finger at Naomi. "She lies! Eglah and all the girls saw her standing idle while my baby was hard at work."

"The orphan is a careless, lazy brat," Hoglah said. "She even tried to keep the widow from doing any work."

Naomi looked into the circle of Hepher's family and saw hatred in every face. She knew then that she and Tirza would always be treated as intruders in this household.

The accusations of the women grew louder until Hepher raised his hand for quiet. "Naomi," he said sternly, "I see that you will have to be taught your place. Do not think you can come into my house and strain the kindness you find here. For your deceitful acts toward my child, you shall be lashed. Let this be your lesson not to tell falsehoods."

In an instant, Hoglah grabbed Naomi's hair, and the women dragged her down the stairs into the house. Michal handed Hoglah the whip.

When she came to, Naomi was alone. The blood had dried on her arms and back, and she trembled with cold. Creeping to her mat next to Tirza's, she whispered to her aunt to wake her, and in the dark, Tirza warmed Naomi's body with her own. Tirza's sobs hurt Naomi more than the whip-lashes.

Long after Tirza fell asleep, the girl who had never known anger was seething with rage. Thoughts she had never before imagined kept her awake and restless. She remembered stories she had heard from travelers around her family's fire, stories of orphaned children who became lawless and roamed the countryside for food. *I will run away and join their band,* she thought. *With them, I can learn to live in the wilderness, steal if I have to, and I will be free, free of this house.*

But hours later, still awake, Naomi knew she couldn't bring dishonor to the names of her parents. And she knew she couldn't run away and leave her aunt. If she deserted her now, Tirza would die bearing the brunt of Naomi's behavior.

I'll repay hate with hate, she vowed to herself. *And my hate will keep me alive until I can take Aunt Tirza away from here.*

Clasping her hands, she prayed. "Eternal One, protector of widows and orphans, keep us strong for the day when we will be free of our oppressors."

But Tirza died before the new moon appeared. The widow at least was free.

Thirteen-year-old Elimelek led his herd of sheep early each morning to drink at the well. Startled by the shouts of younger children, he looked around and saw boys and girls bunched before the opening of a cave. They hurled rocks and stones inside.

"Naomi is a loutish orphan!"

"She tells lies like a beggar!"

"Naomi is dog-lazy! Donkey-lazy! Camel-lazy!"

And a voice called back, "I am not a liar! I am not lazy! I hate you! I hate all of you! You are keeping me from my duty. Uncle's wives will whip me!" But the children responded with more taunts.

Before Elimelek could reach the cave, a young girl leaped out, loosened braids flying, feet kicking, fists flailing. In a pack, the children leaped on her until all Elimelek could see was a pileup of arms and legs.

He pulled off the top combatants. "Go away! Shame on you, fighting one girl! Go away!" He waved his rod at them.

Reluctantly disengaging themselves, the children moved away, some nursing deep scratches. On the ground, the girl still kicked and clawed.

"Stop it," Elimelek said. "Get up, they're gone."

The girl's hair covered her face. Blood oozed from several open wounds. The young shepherd pulled her to her feet, then to the well, where he washed the blood from her legs. Where her dress was torn, he was startled to see black and blue welts.

"What were you thinking of, to start a fight with such a mob?" he asked. "And some of them bigger than you." He pushed aside her tangled hair to wash her bloodied face. "Why, you can't be more than twelve years old, not even my age," he said.

"I'm ten," she sobbed, "and I didn't start the fight. I'm just big for my age."

"Well, why did they start it?"

The girl backed away.

He wondered why she stood with such an air of defiance, shoulders squared, feet planted firmly apart. "Don't be afraid to tell me. My name is Elimelek. I'm your friend."

"I'm not afraid. The fight started because they don't like me."

"Who are they?"

"Sons and daughters of my uncle. I came to live with them after the soldiers killed my father and uncle . . . and took my mother away."

"Oh! Are you the girl who brought the warning?"

"My aunt and I did."

Elimelek had heard about the farm girl who ran from Ephrat under enemy arrows to alert the city while pulling a crying woman along. He had never met a girl who showed the courage of a boy. He looked at her closely. Despite her tangled hair, she had a face that reminded him of his pretty sister, Yocheved.

"I have to get the sheep to pasture," he said. "If your family will let you fetch the night's supply of water, I'll be back by dusk."

Before the sun went down that day, Naomi was waiting at the well for her rescuer. She had already filled the family water-jar and the sheep runnels as well.

"Ho, Naomi!" Elimelek hallooed when he approached her. "Have you been here long?"

"Long enough to have water ready for you and your herd!"

While she poured water for Elimelek into his cupped hands, the sheep nosed thirstily up to the overflowing runnels for their drink.

"It's nice that I don't have to fill the runnels tonight," Elimelek sighed after he had his fill and splashed cool water on his face. "I'm tired. Thank you, Naomi."

"Thank you for helping me this morning," she answered shyly.

"No need." Elimelek looked at her with dark eyes under unruly black hair. "I'm curious about you, you know. That's why I asked you to come back."

"I have no secrets to tell. I live in my uncle's house and will live there until I marry."

Elimelek thought for a moment before he asked his next question. "When a man gives an orphan shelter, he has a right to expect her to be useful. Are you?"

"Yes," she said. "I'm strong. I'm quick, too. My father and mother said I could do more than a son."

"Then why," he asked bluntly, "are your legs and arms so covered with bruises? The children this morning couldn't have put those marks on you."

Naomi didn't answer immediately, but she returned his gaze, weighing and judging him. Elimelek felt that a girl far older than ten was looking at him.

"If you are my friend," she finally said, "then I will tell you. I have these marks because my uncle punished me for his daughter's lies. As for those children this morning, I was not afraid of them. I have fought more than that number."

"More?"

"At the time of the Festival of the First Fruits. Everyone went to the High Priest with their harvests. My uncle's wives said I couldn't go, but I gathered some of my father's first fruits in secret. I followed after the crowd, hidden from Uncle's family. The city children found out and took away my fruits. I fought them all."

"Why did you disobey the order to stay at home?"

"I wanted the High Priest to bless my father's labor, so his name wouldn't be forgotten in Israel."

Elimelek again felt admiration for the girl, but he forced himself to hide it. "An orphan shouldn't behave in such a way. Don't you want your cousins to like you?"

"I want neither cousins nor friends to like me . . . ever . . . except . . . maybe . . ."

"Yes?"

". . . except you."

Elimelek couldn't think of what to say next. "Time to go home," he announced.

The next night Naomi was again waiting for him, water ready. "I'll be at the well every night," she promised him. "I have permission from Uncle's wives, providing we need water for the morning."

"I may not be here every night, Naomi. When I have duties in the fields and orchards, then my brothers are in charge of the sheep."

The girl's face fell.

Elimelek said softly, "Wait to see what each day brings. Perhaps it will bring joy."

She smiled. "I haven't felt joy since Aunt Tirza died. But with you, I will try."

Elimelek thought Naomi's smile transformed her entire being.

Their meetings at the well became the highlight of Naomi's days and she lived for the minutes she spent with the young shepherd. The weeks flew by. Soon Elimelek said, "The hot sun of summer has shriveled the herbage. Tomorrow I take the herd to the distant hills for pasturage. I'll be back before the autumn rains, in a few months."

"I'll be waiting for you," Naomi said quietly.

With her young shepherd gone, Naomi moved woodenly through the routine of her days. She welcomed the work piled on her, glad to fall into exhausted sleep at night, so as not to think of Elimelek.

Before the early autumn rains fell, he returned. And she was waiting for him at the well, water ready.

"Ho, Naomi! Have you been here long?" he hallooed.

"Long enough to have water ready for you and your herd!"

They smiled at each other as if he had been gone only a day, and he held out his hands for her to pour the cool water in them. Refreshed, he looked at her closely.

"You have grown thinner."

"I've been lonely," she answered simply.

"What did you do while I was gone?"

"The same as ever, except that there haven't been any fights. The city children don't call me names anymore. They don't dare!"

He laughed. "You may be thinner, but you haven't changed. You're just waiting for a challenge."

She put her hand in his. Then they both laughed, glad that the long separation was over.

The years passed swiftly, and as he did every midsummer Elimelek sought greener pastures for his herd. When he returned, after long months of solitary sheepherding, he said to Naomi, "I confess that for the first time I found myself wishing for someone to talk with. You are spoiling me. I am getting dependent on your company."

He could see the happiness in her eyes at what he had said, so he teased her by saying, "You must not come to the well anymore. I must keep my independence."

And just as quickly he could see the chill that came into her eyes. "I didn't mean it," he said. "Let's talk of other things . . . what have you been thinking while I was gone?"

Naomi sighed. "I don't have time to think. I carry dung to the fields after I've cleaned the cattle pens. I help Uncle's hired men remove the rocks from new fields. I build fences with the rocks and prepare the land for planting. In the vineyards, I clear the vines, and in the olive groves, I beat the trees—"

Elimelek interrupted her. "So, that's why you're growing so tall. You've developed a long stretch!"

She responded with a faint smile. Why should she tell him that every day she had to guard against the men who sometimes tried to put their hands on her body? They had learned to leave her alone. The men called her "wildcat" and had the scars to prove it. She knew that Elimelek would never suspect the threats she faced.

At fifteen, Naomi was not attractive by the standards of the Judean and Canaanite women of Bethlehem. She was not petite and dainty. She did not make flattering conversation. She did not behave coquettishly, flirting with veiled eyes, walking with a swaying motion so that little bells on her wrists and ankles might tinkle, as was the fashion.

But Naomi had heavy, brown braids that were a crown befitting her tall, straight carriage. She walked with the grace of a lioness, her slow movements concealing taut muscles, alert to danger. And when she was threatened, her eyes glittered with green flecks. Only her full, curved lips hinted at the tenderness inside.

She managed to keep her love for Elimelek from everyone, even from him. Each day she prayed he would sense her true feelings toward him. Her constant thought was, *How can I make him know? What can I do to make him aware?*

The answer came unexpectedly.

CHAPTER 3

It was late summer. Elimelek was usually working in the fields to harvest the crops, but his brother Shmuel's wife, Zilpah, was nearing her time to give birth, so Elimelek took over the sheepherding duties. When he returned with the herd, he was not surprised to find Naomi waiting at the well.

"I know I've said it many times, Naomi, but after a hot day on the hillside without a tent or bush to give shade, I can't wait until I see the trees outside Bethlehem."

He glanced around as he splashed cool water on his face and hands. "The well is deserted. Where is everyone?"

"Gone home. You don't realize how late it is."

"So it is," he said. "But I need a rest before going home myself. Refill your water jar and bring it to the rise where we can sit for a while."

As they rested on the slope of the land and looked down over the sheep that drank thirstily from the water runnels Naomi had filled.

Elimelek stretched out on the ground, head pillowed on his arms, eyes closed. "This is a wonderful country, Naomi. I love every part of it. Can you smell the air? It smells even better up in the mountains. In all the world, there can be no more beautiful land than ours. When you marry, prevail on your husband to show you all that the Eternal One gave our ancestors."

Softly, Naomi asked, "Whom will I marry?" but Elimelek didn't hear her.

"You'll see fertile plains, freshwater springs and waterfalls, ponds swarming with fish, vineyards and orchards, mountainsides covered with grassy meadows, and towering cedar and pine trees. Oh, Naomi! Even the desolate wildness of Judah's rocky hills is magnificent."

"You savor our country as you would a ripe apricot," she said.

"I can't help it. When my family sits together every Sabbath and every festival, my father repeats the story of the Israelites' deliverance from slavery in Egypt; he makes me love my country, my religion, and my people."

Naomi looked at the relaxed figure beside her. At the age of eighteen, Elimelek was a seasoned farmer and sheepherder whose work demanded stamina, strength, and courage. The short garment he wore exposed the hard muscles of his arms and legs. The wide cloth belt around his waist held a shepherd's flute and a slingshot. A scrip bag for food and a leather bottle for water hung from his neck. His half-closed eyes were the same black as his thick hair and beard. Naomi wondered how Elimelek could be so attuned to homeland, family, and faith, and still be so blind to her love.

She turned her gaze to the bluish-pink sky. In the serenity of the twilight hour, she heard only the contented baaing of the sheep and the twittering of the birds.

Elimelek opened his eyes and squeezed Naomi's hand. "Also, ask your husband to show you—"

She turned to him.

Elimelek saw the pensiveness in her face, the softness in her eyes, and something more that made him feel warm inside. The scent of field flowers carried by the evening breeze enveloped him.

"Ask my husband to show me what?"

Unaccountably, he forgot what he was going to say. A strange, happy excitement was creeping over him. He became conscious of their aloneness and drew his hand away.

"Nothing."

But when she wasn't looking, he stole a sidelong glance at her. Why did she disturb him tonight? She was, after all, the same Naomi. She wore the same coarsely woven, threadbare dress tied at the waist with a piece of rope. Yet tonight, she was different. Even her tanned, olive skin and heavy unbound braids gleamed with hidden lights. He wondered what it would be like to kiss her.

And then a random, icy thought crossed his mind. "Naomi! How did you know I would be here tonight?"

She turned to him again but didn't answer. The truth was that she had waited for him every night.

"Only this morning Shmuel and I changed places," Elimelek said. "I hadn't known, when I last saw you, that I would be shepherd today. How did you know?"

"Oh, I knew you would be here," she teased. "Those birds up in the tree said to me, 'Don't go home yet, Naomi. That Elimelek, the one who makes music with a reed pipe, had to work as a shepherd today. Why don't you get water ready for his return?' "

Elimelek searched her eyes.

The girl's smile faded, puzzled by the chilling intensity of his gaze.

Deliberately he turned his back to her, his face to the lowering sun. "I am not jesting, Naomi. It is unseemly for you to come here by yourself."

He paused, realizing this was an awkward thing to say. The social life of the young men and women of Bethlehem centered at the well. In the morning and early evening, they met and chatted there while drawing water for livestock and household needs.

Unaware that love and jealousy had overtaken him so swiftly, Elimelek was besieged by conflicting emotions. "If we are seen here alone at this late hour," he began, "people will talk. Since you are an orphan, you must take care that your conduct is above reproach. You have no family to defend your reputation."

Having started, he couldn't stop himself. "Do you come here to have late meetings with other men as well?"

Naomi stiffened with shock. What was Elimelek saying? Was this the same boy she had loved from the day he came into her life? She couldn't think. She didn't know what she had said or done to deserve this outburst from him. Anger, humiliation, unrequited love churned within her. She shut her eyes tightly to hold back the tears. An expressionless mask slipped over her face. Now she knew: to Elimelek, as to all others in her bleak world, she was an ugly, unwanted orphan.

He was still talking, face averted.

"You should never come here again to meet me. I am a man ready for marriage as soon as my father buys me a wife from a house where my family can gain by the marriage."

Aghast at his own words, he wanted a response from her, yet he didn't dare to look at her.

Silently, Naomi rose, pulled up the water jar, settled it on her head, and began to thread her way up the stony path to the city.

Elimelek got up hurriedly, stumbling over the stones. "Naomi! Come back!"

He reached up and swung her around. Naomi's hold on the jar was so firm that she didn't let go but fell backward, the water spilling in a shower over Elimelek below. Water streamed in rivulets from his hair, over his face, down his tunic front into the flute at his waist. The sight was so ludicrous, Naomi couldn't help laughing where she lay on the ground.

Elimelek was sputtering. "It is bad enough you don't know how to behave, coming here alone to meet men—"

Naomi sat up, the laughter gone. Rage ignited green sparks in her eyes. "How dare you? How dare you accuse me of such things? How dare you speak so to me!"

She sprang at him, her fingers tearing viciously at his face and neck. She was wild with hurt: hurt at Elimelek's insults, hurt that her love was mistaken and her trust misused, hurt at her lowly status and the abuse she received daily in her uncle's house, hurt that her life was devoid of hope. Elimelek was the man she loved, yet at this moment he symbolized everything hateful in her life.

Elimelek knew the strength of an enraged Naomi: even though he was taller and stronger than she was, those clawing fingernails could rip his flesh and blind his eyes. He threw her down on her back. Gouging his knee into her abdomen, he knocked the breath from her. She lay still, stunned by the fall and blow. Quickly he removed his knee and watched anxiously as her face paled, the blood receding under the brown of her skin.

"Naomi, please . . . are you all right? Say you are all right. Naomi?"

Slipping his arm under her shoulders, he sat her up, helping to get air back into her lungs. He held her close against him, raising her to her feet. She gasped, coughed, gasped again until she could draw deep breaths of air.

When finally she could speak, she struggled out of his arms. "Don't touch me! Don't ever come near me!"

She snatched up the overturned water pitcher. Painfully arching her back as she moved, she returned to the well.

CHAPTER
4

Uncertain what to do, Elimelek whistled to the lead ram to get the sheep moving. As he walked with them up the path to the highway, he tried to sort out his jumbled feelings: in the short while that he had sat beside her, he had discovered his desire to be with Naomi, but he had also discovered his jealousy. He had fought with Naomi when what he really wanted was to hold her in his arms.

Elimelek knew Naomi was brave to fight him. What pride of character she had to resent his insults! She was not like other girls who behaved amorously to arouse desire in boys, then ran home like scared mice. He had never seen Naomi flirt.

He smiled ruefully. Of course, the young people shunned her as a fighting spitfire. Poor Naomi. How would she ever get a husband? What man would see the loving and gentle side of her?

Suddenly he felt apprehension. Naomi married to some man, aged and tyrannical perhaps? But why should *he* be concerned? *Her uncle will not let her marry, not while her father's farm gives him good profits. Of course my family would never consider . . . I wonder . . . I wonder if I dare . . .*

"Elimelek! Elimelek!"

Startled, he heard the elders of the city calling him. He was now inside the gates, following the herd through the marketplace.

"Ho! Hear! Elimelek, why are you so late tonight?

"Did you find a new field? Is there good grazing?"

"Tell your father to come to the gates tonight. We have matters of great urgency to discuss. We're waiting for him."

The gates of Bethlehem and the marketplace were one. The thick wall surrounding the city overlapped on the southern side so that an area forty feet wide was left open in between. This was the only free space in the city. The square opening was also the entranceway, barred by huge wooden gates that were locked each night. Attackers trying to storm the gates were ambushed in the marketplace; from the top of the stone wall, arrows and hot oil streamed down on the enemy. Here also the ruling body for the city, the Council of Elders, held court on stone benches.

At this late hour, the traders were absent but the square hummed with activity. Elimelek took no notice of the laborers waiting to be hired for the next day, the scribes sitting cross-legged with their quills and papyrus rolls, the mercenaries looking for overnight lodging, or the beggars squabbling among themselves.

Again lost in thought, he followed his herd past the Street of the Bakers, the Street of the Potters, the other business streets, and the wine merchants. Beyond this district was the maze of narrow, unpaved roads where the houses and yards pushed against each other so closely that the streets were only crooked passageways. The mud and stone homes were much the same, with their canopied porches on the flat rooftops. In back of the houses were the cattle enclosures. The front yards served as outdoor kitchens, dining rooms, and work rooms. The whole was surrounded by waist-high stone fences.

Bethlehem's large families were completely self-sufficient: they produced and made everything they wore, ate, and used. Flat rounds of bread, which took hours to make because flour had to be milled fresh every day, were the mainstay of life. Fruits and vegetables were plentiful, but families ate little meat because Israel's herds were too important to the economy of the small nation to be used for daily food.

Elimelek dragged his feet. He was bewildered. He knew now that he was in love, and with someone who would not be welcome in his father's house.

"Son! Son! Where are you going?"

Elimelek had walked right past his father, Nathan, who was standing inside the gate of their yard.

"Oh! Good evening, Father. Is everyone in already?"

"In and counted, even the sheep."

They smiled at each other, the handsome boy and the portly, white-haired man. Natan was short but dignified, and his decisive manner marked him as a man of authority, a patriarch in Israel. His children and grandchildren felt his love as well as his discipline. He was the source of strength that united his Hezronite family.

"Father, after the meal I want a word with you . . . alone."

"Alone?"

"Yes, I want to talk to you about some things I have on my mind."

"I'm glad you do," Natan teased, "else I would suspect your mind had been affected by today's hot sun."

Elimelek laughed, then remembered the message from the elders. "Father, there will be a meeting of the council tonight. You are needed there."

Just then Elimelek's mother—Malkah—and his brothers' wives—Aviah, Rahav, and Zilpah—came out of the house carrying bowls of food and pitchers of wine and milk. "Come, everyone, Elimelek's home!" they called as they placed the food on woven mats on the ground.

From the rooftop, Elimelek's brothers Benyamin, Mattityahu, and Shmuel clambered down, along with nephews and nieces of assorted ages and sizes.

"We have been waiting ever so long!"

"I'm hungry!"

"We eat! We eat!" they chorused.

"Anything happen to delay you?" asked Shmuel, who was closest to Elimelek in age and companionship.

Elimelek commented tersely, "I see that Zilpah is here, serving instead of giving birth."

Adults and children seated themselves in a circle around the food-laden mats. Natan lived as his ancestors did: when his wife, sons, and son's families gathered around him, he rejoiced and thanked God for all the blessings they enjoyed. As soon as the men and children had their bowls filled, the women sat down with them. This family meal was the highlight of the day for all of them.

I wonder how Naomi would see our home for the first time, Elimelek thought as he ate.

Facing the entrance gate was his parents' dwelling, the one-story home in which Elimelek and his siblings had been born. As each son married, Natan erected a similar house for the newlyweds. The three additional homes decreased the size of the yard considerably, but there was yet one space left for Elimelek's house.

Natan's choices of brides for his sons were fortunate ones. The fifty shekels he had paid each girl's family was a fair price to pay for loving daughters. Their fathers had not kept the money that was rightfully theirs for having relinquished a useful member in their homes, but instead bestowed the gold on their daughters as wedding gifts. Thus, each girl brought to her husband tables, chairs, mats, pots, mills, and clothing to furnish the new home. Since each couple had its own quarters, Natan's household was peaceful.

Elimelek studied his brothers and their wives. *How would Naomi, without dowry or kin, fit into our family?*

He gazed at his mother. Malkah's matronly figure was like a symbol of providence. From her, all good things flowed. He knew her heart was wide and that she alone might welcome the woman Elimelek loved.

His eyes lingered on his father. As wise and understanding of people as he was, he might object to Naomi.

But, the more he considered the objections his family would raise, the more Elimelek was determined to have Naomi . . . and soon. In this troubling time, when the Hebrews' hold on their country was still weak, Elimelek knew it was important for a man to marry young and beget sons. The cycles of famine, disease, and battle to protect the land took a toll on young men. If a man could afford it, he took more than one wife to ensure many sons. Marriages were arranged to bring families and tribes together for mutual gain and safety. Marriages were not arranged for love.

The meal over, the grandchildren pulled Natan to his feet.

"And what now, you mischievous ones?" he growled playfully.

Natan loved all of his grandchildren but he was especially drawn to the little girls. He missed his first-born child, his only daughter, Yocheved, who had married ten years before and gone to live with her Danite husband, Hanoch, in his faraway city in the North. Natan had not seen her since her wedding day, but Hanoch came to Bethlehem twice a year with his donkey caravan to trade the merchandise he had bought from Phoenician merchants for Bethlehemite wool. Natan was proud of Hanoch's business acumen and welcomed him joyfully, but he longed to see his daughter, knowing full well that she was busy rearing a growing family of six children while managing a wool bazaar. Deprived of Yocheved's sunny presence, Natan was unusually indulgent to his granddaughters.

"Is this the way to treat your *sabah*?" he asked. He pretended helplessness as they searched his wide cloth belt for sweets. "Don't you know who wears the hat of authority here?" They squealed with delight as he tickled them.

"Father!" Elimelek's voice rose above the din. "Please, Father."

His brothers looked at him. "Hold your noise. What do you want of Father?"

Elimelek started to rebuke them but thought better of it. He needed their consent, too.

"I will tell you if you get the children off Father. I have a matter to discuss."

Natan set the children down. "Yes, son, we will have our talk alone."

As he saw his brothers rise, Elimelek said, "It's all right, Father. I'm asking my brothers to come, too."

They climbed the outside stairs to the canopied rooftop, where it was cool and quiet, away from the women and the children.

"Father," Elimelek began nervously, "tell me, have you found a suitable wife for me yet?"

The four listeners smiled broadly. Natan said, "Why, yes, we have found several who would be excellent matches. Your brothers and I know the families well. We have been discussing the terms of payments each family demands before we decide on the one."

"Don't be a fidget," Shmuel laughed. "We'll get you one soon enough."

"Why the sudden interest in a wife?" Benyamin asked.

"I'm not a fidget," Elimelek said. "It's just . . . I've decided that I want to select the woman I'm going to marry."

"What?"

"Why the change of mind?" asked Mattityahu. "Only a few days ago when we spoke of it, you showed no interest and said our judgment was best.

"Father!" Elimelek appealed, "must I always have Benyamin or Mattityahu do my thinking for me? Why can't I change my mind?"

"I don't understand your sudden sharpness with your brothers," Natan replied. "I, too, am curious at your new attitude. Tell us what's on your mind."

"I want to marry someone of my own choosing . . ."

"Well, who is she?" Natan asked. "Do we know her family?"

Elimelek took a breath. "Yes, you know her family. She is Naomi, niece of Hepher the Hamulite."

"No!"

"Not she!"

"Never!"

Natan, trying to place the girl, asked, "Is she the daughter of the murdered Jashuv and the enslaved Merav?"

The brothers' voices rose. "He means the giantess! That ungainly niece of Hepher's!"

"He's talking about the fighting vixen!"

"How can Elimelek pick such a misfit for a wife?"

The brothers knew Naomi had no father or brother, no males of wealth to enforce interfamily ties, no outstanding beauty or talent to add to a family's prestige. She had only a reputation as a troublemaker.

"We won't have her!"

"She'll fight with our women."

"What can you possibly gain if you marry her? She'll only bring discord among us!"

Natan watched Elimelek's face turn red with anger. Already he had changed from a docile boy to a resolute man. The father quieted his sons by raising his hand for silence.

"Elimelek, my son, we know you must have given careful thought to this request. Since we are all involved in your marriage, tell us why you want this girl."

The young man searched for the right words. His reasons had to be practical; he knew he couldn't mention love.

"I want Naomi for my wife because she is strong and will work for our benefit. I know she can be bought with a small payment because her uncle has too many women in his household. A sheep or two would be enough."

He paused. What he had said was only a guess. "I have known Naomi since she came to live in Bethlehem and I would rather have her than someone I do not know. That is all."

The brothers looked at each other in dismay. They rose and stamped down the stairs.

Elimelek looked at his father imploringly.

"I must leave for the council meeting," Natan said. "We'll talk about this further after your brothers and I give thought to your request."

"But, Father! What is there to think about? I don't care if my brothers found families with rich daughters. I will have the bride I choose!"

"Elimelek!" Natan was stern. "I will not tolerate disrespect from my youngest son toward his brothers. You will wait and accept our decision."

He left Elimelek sitting alone, dejected at having been treated like a child, and fearful of having lost his chance to wed Naomi.

That night when Natan returned home, he discussed Elimelek's future with Malkah.

"My husband," she said, "our sons' reasons for not wanting Naomi are valid. But, each of them had the final say in the selection of his bride and each gained happiness. So why should they deny Elimelek his right to choose his own bride? Naomi must be an exceptional girl if Elimelek wants her without any worldly goods."

"But aren't you afraid that having Naomi here will bring strife into our family?" Natan asked.

Malkah considered. "Just as our daughters-in-law, with different personalities, adjusted to each other, so they'll adjust to Naomi, and Naomi to them."

Natan was relieved. Unlike some fathers of his generation, he wanted his sons to be as contented in their marriages as he was in his. He didn't suspect that in her heart Malkah had misgivings.

Malkah knew she had simplified the matter too much: it took a long time for strong personalities to mellow and to accommodate. Yet, she also knew that a withdrawn, unhappy Elimelek would be harder for her to bear than a contentious Naomi.

Natan said, "I have no objections to Naomi, since she is of good parentage. I believe her father's property, small as it is, has grown to considerable value. Well, we'll see what her uncle will want."

As she limped back to the well to refill the pitcher, Naomi heard Elimelek whistle to his herd, but she forced herself not to look back or to think of him. She had to return to the city before the gates closed for the night.

Michal, sitting in the doorway, greeted her. "Why are you so late coming home? I think Hepher should know."

Naomi said nothing. The bowls and cups on the table were all turned over, piled one on top of the other, cleaned of food. Filling the reserve water jar to the top, Naomi covered it and set the remainder on the table. She went to the women's bedroom, unrolled her mat, and eased herself down on it. Both her body and heart ached. She closed her eyes, but not to sleep.

She hated herself. What did Elimelek think of her, attacking him in such a rage? She was tormented with shame.

Eternal One, she prayed, *when Aunt Tirza died, I wanted to die, too. Then You sent me Elimelek, and I have lived in hope, waiting for him to love me. Now I have lost the only one in this world I love. Please, give me a sign. Show me what to do.*

The tears slid from her eyes as she turned her face to the wall.

A week later Natan paid Hepher a visit. It was the Sabbath and the master of the house was resting on the rooftop. The women were indoors and the sons were meeting friends at the town gates. Only the grandchildren were in the yard, observing the Sabbath in quiet play. Respectfully, one grand-son opened the gate for Natan, while another ran up the stairs to inform his grandfather of the unexpected visitor.

When he saw Natan standing in the yard, dressed in his Sabbath best, Hepher smiled his surprise and waved him up. When they were face to face, they bowed courteously to each other.

Natan and Hepher were kinsmen, belonging to the Perezite clan of Bethlehem-Ephrat. Both men were powerful, active members of the ruling

Council of Elders and both were wealthy patriarchs of large families.

The host motioned his guest to a seat under the canopy. "I am honored to have you spend the Sabbath with me. Permit me to offer the hospitality of my house. A little wine, perhaps?"

Goblet in hand, Natan opened the conversation casually. "I have heard that trouble is brewing with the Philistines in the North again. My daughter's husband traveled through here two days ago and brought us the news."

"Yes, I heard it, too," said Hepher, "but I am more concerned with trouble closer to home."

"The Amalekites?"

"Yes. Of all our enemies, I hate them the most. They were the ones who murdered my brothers Jashuv and Machir."

"Then you have thought of retribution for their deaths?"

Hepher grew uncomfortable at the turn of the conversation. What was the real purpose of Natan's visit? Testily, he answered, "Of course. For many years my sons and I have talked of the need for unity between the tribes to avenge the deaths of all our murdered men."

"And what did you decide?"

Hepher shrugged. "Our conclusion is always the same. We Judeans are not strong enough to set up an army to patrol all of Judah."

"True. What do you think should be the next step?"

"We must have armies in every tribe, with God-inspired men to lead them."

"And who will appoint a captain over the leaders?" Natan asked. "We need one strong man to hold the armies in check, using them only for patrol and defense."

"No!" Hepher said angrily. "I will never consent to electing one man to control the armies. He would have the power of a king or a pharaoh. I told the council many times that I am against putting a king over me. I say to you, too, Natan, that as an elder in Bethlehem, I will never take orders from a king!"

"I, too, hate the thought of a king," Natan answered. "A king would have the power to lead us into war for his own gain, but our survival depends on uniting. If we fail to bind ourselves under one man's leadership, each tribe will be conquered one at a time, and someday Judah's men will be slaves again."

Hepher's eyes gleamed. "If only I were a younger man, I would lead our men into battle!"

Natan shook his head. There were so many men like Hepher, afraid of the Amalekites, the Egyptians, and the rest, yet more afraid of losing their own petty authority.

Natan decided to change the subject. In an offhand way, he said, "You spoke of your two brothers. How old now is the daughter left by Jashuv?"

So! This is the reason for his visit, Hepher thought. "My niece is fifteen, soon to be sixteen years old."

"That old? Has she been asked for in marriage?"

Hepher hesitated. If he said that others wanted Naomi, he might wangle a fat payment for himself. But if the price were too high, Natan might refuse to consider the girl.

He began in a mournful voice, "Alas, my brother's child has been my care and my expense for many years . . ."

"I am sure that you have performed your duty as an uncle responsibly. Should anyone ask for her, what would be the marriage terms?"

Hepher's eyes narrowed. "Who will take her?"

"My youngest son, Elimelek."

"Five ewes, ten shekels, and her father's property."

Natan almost smiled at the swiftness of Hepher's response. "It is against the law for you to keep her father's property after she marries," he pointed out. "I offer no money, just three ewes."

"What? Three ewes? How can you make such an offer? After all the years I have taken care of her? It's like taking away a man worker!"

Natan said dryly, "I understand that you have received excellent profit every year from her father's farm. Three ewes only."

Hepher considered. "It's midsummer," he said, "and I know it's your custom to send your son and your herd to the hills for pasturage. Agree to let me keep the farm until your son returns."

"As you say, let it be."

"Three unblemished ewes and the property until your son claims it."

"So be it."

Hepher held out his palm and Natan struck it, thus binding the contract.

Elimelek waited anxiously for Natan.

"Well, Father, what happened?"

"Hepher wants three unblemished ewes."

Elimelek was shocked. "Was that all? He didn't ask for money?"

"Of course he did. But you said he would let Naomi go for a sheep or two, so I offered three and he accepted."

"Will he give Naomi anything? Doesn't she have an inheritance?"

"Hepher insists on keeping her father's property until you return at the end of the summer."

"But, Father! I can't have Naomi shamed by coming here empty-handed. My brothers' wives will look down on her!"

Natan looked at his son in surprise.

Elimelek read the look. "It's my right to give Naomi some wedding jewelry," he said defensively. "Will you and my brothers grant me money?"

"Knowing how your brothers feel about her, I will say no to your request. The money belongs to all of us, true, but since your brothers have put in the greater share, they will refuse you."

"But they bought jewelry for their wives!"

"Their wives were welcomed by all and they brought large dowries."

That night, Elimelek sat apart from the others. After a while he felt the soft arm of his mother around his shoulders.

"Elimelek," she said, "you ate no supper."

"I wasn't hungry."

"I see you're unhappy."

Elimelek sighed, "Mother, I'm not ashamed to tell you this. I love Naomi. I don't want her pride hurt more than it is already. I know Father is right to deny me money for gifts, but I, too, have pride. I want to give my wife something beautiful."

"Then you will. When I left my father's house to marry, he gave me two bracelets, without jewels, but made of finest gold. You may have them for your bride."

The boy threw his arms around his mother. "Oh, Mother, you do understand! You will make Naomi proud!"

The following Sabbath Naomi was summoned to her uncle's presence. She wondered what she had done.

"You are most fortunate today, Naomi."

"Yes, Uncle?"

"I have arranged a marriage for you."

By habit she held an expressionless mask on her face, but this time, her heart also turned to stone. What old man had her uncle found as husband for her? Only an old man, rich in herds and wives, would listen to Hepher's request to take his strong niece as a third or fourth wife to aid ailing spouses, burdened with too many children or not enough children.

Hepher ignored her silence. "You are pledged to the family of Natan, the Hezronite. Of his four sons, you will be taken by his youngest, Elimelek."

Naomi dropped her eyes. She dared not let Hepher see her joy or he might change his mind. She controlled the excitement that shook her entire being, the song that came to her lips.

Lowering her voice, she asked, "When am I to go?"

Hepher accepted her calmness as a sign of resignation. "Elimelek will take you tonight. Tomorrow he leaves with his herd."

"Yes, Uncle." She waited.

"I have been generous with you," Hepher added. "At great cost to myself I have kept your father's land from lying idle. When Elimelek and you return, I will offer to buy the land from your husband."

"Uncle, I don't presume to know, but shouldn't my husband's family receive my inheritance when I enter their house?"

Hepher's answer was biting. "I am not required to tell you the terms of the purchase, but since I have accepted such a small amount from Natan, the agreement is that the land remains with me until your husband is ready to work on it."

Naomi flushed with humiliation. She would have to go to Elimelek's house as a pauper.

"I am giving you a wedding present: your marriage veil. Now make yourself ready. As soon as the Sabbath is over at sundown, Elimelek will be here. My household and I bid you farewell."

Hepher rose and without a backward glance left his niece. Naomi stood there, reflecting. This was her wedding benediction from the man who was supposed to have taken her father's place, the blood relative whose words, "May you soon be the mother of many sons" she had once hoped to hear. The five work-filled years spent in his house elicited no more than an indifferent farewell, no invitation ever to return to see him.

She looked at the sky. The sun would soon be down.

Hoglah, Michal, their daughters, daughters-in-law, and granddaughters were lounging in the women's bedroom. They already knew of Naomi's coming marriage, but no one spoke to her or offered to help her prepare for this great event in her life.

Nor did Naomi ask for help. She filled a basin with water, untied her braids, and bending low over the basin, began to wash her long hair.

Watching her every move, the women addressed each other.

"My mother washed my hair with rose-leaf scented water on my wedding day."

"My mother cried all the while she washed my hair. I cried too, because I knew she loved me and was sad to see me leave."

Avishag said, "Father has promised me an alabaster box filled with spikenard herbs and many jewels, so that I won't be impatient to marry. He doesn't want to see me leave because he loves me most."

Naomi paid no attention. Once, these taunting remarks would have made her fly into a rage and cry out, "My father loved me! My mother loved me! They would have given me gifts, too!" And for such insolence the older women would have beaten her. Having been subjected to the ox-goad and whip so many times, Naomi had learned to hold her tongue.

One daughter-in-law broke in, "Have you seen the ribbons I wore in my hair when I came here as a bride?"

She went to her carved wooden chest and brought out a handful of colored ribbons for her husband's family to admire. The young girls crowded around, exclaiming and sighing over them.

Naomi twisted her hair to dry it. She knew they had seen the ribbons time and again, and when they were bored with looking they had fought over them. Her damp hair coiled on her head, Naomi threw the water out and refilled the basin with fresh water.

Eglah commented angrily, "She no longer has to draw water so she throws out a good basinful!"

With quiet defiance, Naomi untied the rope from her waist, slipped off the dress, and washed every part of her body.

"What a monstrous-shaped wretch Elimelek will discover he has taken to wife!" remarked Michal.

"She looks as though she could be the mother to oxen, not sons." Hoglah's comment convulsed the women with laughter.

But hatred clouded the women's vision. Naomi without clothes was a figure of superb womanhood. Her lithe figure was as brown and smooth as an Egyptian pillar. She was slender, yet her body had the perfected fullness of maturity.

Now Avishag slipped off her clothes and with mimicking gestures pretended to be washing herself. The women shrieked at the comparison of Naomi's movements with Avishag's exaggeratedly clownish ones. Gleefully, the little granddaughters caught the spirit of spite and pranced about, grimacing as they followed Avishag's lead.

Naomi picked up her dress, brushed it thoroughly, and put it back on.

"Did you ever see my mantle with gold thread around the neck and sleeves?" asked another daughter-in-law, as she ran to pull it out of her clothes box.

"My parents presented me with a heavy wool mantle for the cold days. It was embroidered with red and purple flowers," said another as she hurried to get it.

This was the signal for elegant dresses and coats to be spread about, vying for the bride's attention and envy.

Naomi ignored the show staged for her. Carefully, she folded over the worn-out places in the dress, then tied the rope tightly around her waist to keep the folds in place. From a niche in the wall she took out her only pair of shoes, brushed them, and put them on. Finally, she combed her shining hair into two neat braids. She was dressed for her wedding.

Hoglah grudgingly tossed her a white, loosely woven square of wool. "Here is your bridal veil from my husband."

Naomi caught the scarf. It was the first beautiful thing she had received since her arrival in Bethlehem. She smoothed it gently, tears springing to her eyes. None of the women's jibes and sneers hurt as much as the contrast of the white veil with her own worn-out dress. How she yearned to adorn herself in luxurious clothes for Elimelek's admiration, to be breathtakingly lovely for him.

When Naomi swung the white covering over her head, the women scrambled to follow suit, except that over their veils they affixed wedding crowns, ornate jeweled circles hung with gold coins. Posturing and strutting, they billowed out the veils, the crowns held in place. They bent their heads this way and that, the better to examine each other's costly headpieces.

Naomi stood silently watching them, untouched by their demonstrations. And when it was finally obvious to them that nothing they had said or done had aroused her, their fun was suddenly flat and the show ended.

Naomi said in a quiet voice, "Hoglah, I thank my uncle for his wedding gift."

Then, looking into the eyes of each of them, she added, "My uncle has arranged for me to marry and leave tonight. When I came here five years ago I offered you my love but you didn't want it. You found me at fault because I was an orphan in need of my uncle's protection. I thank him for the shelter of his house. I thank you for nothing. I will not see any of you again."

Naomi looked around the room. There was nothing she had forgotten because there was nothing she owned. As a child she had come to Hepher's house with only the clothes she wore. She was leaving it with little more than that.

The sun was gone. The Sabbath was over. Carefully, Naomi adjusted the veil over her face. She walked to the outer doorway, the women crowding after her in a silent cluster.

CHAPTER
6

Already Elimelek was standing at Hepher's gate, alone except for three ewes.

To Naomi, he was a dazzling sight: over a snowy white shirt and long, loose trousers he wore a voluminous cloak of purple-and-white striped wool edged with black fringe. A turban of the same cloth was wound around his head.

The regal attire concealed his trembling body. Elimelek's anxiety had begun the previous Sabbath when he waited impatiently for his father to complete the first half of the marriage—the offer and acceptance of the contract between Hepher and Natan.

The second half of the marriage was the act of leading Naomi from her house to his after the payment of the three ewes.

Now he stood before Hepher's yard, feeling last minute qualms. What if he had made a mistake? Naomi had told him never to see her. Did she really mean it or was she simply speaking in the anger of the moment?

Hepher was opening the gate, eyes on the sheep. It was too late for Elimelek to turn back.

"Welcome, son of Natan," Hepher said. "I see you have brought the payment." He knelt on the road to examine the animals closely.

"These are the finest of our herd, without blemish," Elimelek said.

"Yes," said Hepher, pleased. "You have honored the contract. I accept the payment."

They bowed formally and the new owner led the ewes to the sheep fold in the back, leaving the gate ajar for Elimelek to enter the yard and claim his bride.

Naomi was waiting in the doorway, her head covered with the white scarf. She had stopped breathing while Hepher inspected the sheep. She feared that if they had one little sore, Hepher would refuse the payment. She was too close to freedom and love to have something happen now. Her lips moved in silent prayer. Only when she saw the two men bow to each

33

other did she breathe again. And not until Elimelek crossed the yard and stood before her did she unlock her fingers.

She waited, trembling, for him to nod and lead the way out. Elimelek could not see Naomi's face, but he could see the tension in her tightly knotted fingers. He reached for her hands and from a pocket in his mantle withdrew two glistening gold bracelets. As he slipped them over her wrists, the women behind Naomi let out gasps of surprise.

Naomi was overcome. Blessedly, the veil hid her tears. With the bracelets, Elimelek had placed a high value on her in front of the people who had most demeaned her.

Elimelek, properly, did not remove the veil covering his bride's face, but turned and walked out of the yard with Naomi a few steps behind, his acknowledged wife. As he strode through the streets, he contrasted his marriage to those of his brothers. In their cases, as soon as the purchase terms had been agreed on between the fathers, Natan and Malkah had invited the wedding guests. Preparations for the seven-day feast were begun weeks ahead. Then, on the day the groom walked to the bride's house, his entire family accompanied him, surrounded by musicians playing cymbals, lyre, and flutes. Hired professional singers sang of the bridegroom's great strength in field and battle; they sang of the magnificence of the payment his family made for the bride; they sang of the numbers and prowess of the sons he would father to keep his name alive in Israel; they sang of the plenteous wedding feast awaiting the invited guests.

To the bride they sang:
Fair and comely is the bride to look upon.
A mother of many will she be.
May God grant her many sons.
Blessed will be her name in Israel.

And as the wedding procession wound its way back to Natan's house, bystanders congratulated or teased the bridal couple: often the remarks were ribald, which set the mood for the feasting and merriment that continued for days.

Elimelek knew his wedding celebration would not be like his brothers' and he didn't care. When he, followed by Naomi, arrived at his parents' gate, only his own family awaited them.

"Blessings to the groom and bride," Natan and Malkah called out.

"Welcome to Naomi, wife of our son."

The brothers and wives chorused the same while the children skittered around the bride, eager to see her face under the veil.

With a smile, Elimelek waved the children aside as he strode to his father's house. Opening the door, he waited for Naomi to enter, then he closed it firmly.

Natan's house was different from Hepher's many-roomed one. This house was one great room with three levels. Half the room was occupied by a long table and stools. Against one wall stood farm equipment, including stone mangers filled with straw used as beds for newborn lambs and goats. The mangers had once served as cradles for Malkah's babies.

The second level was a raised platform where Natan and Malkah slept. In the rear of the platform stood tall reserve jars filled with water, oil, grain, and the staples of Malkah's panty. On the shelves were baskets of all sizes.

Against the far wall were steps leading up to the third level, which was the loft where Elimelek and his brothers had slept when they were children. Naomi's veil did not obscure her view and she was looking around with interest when she realized that Elimelek was holding out his hand. She put her hand in his. He led her up the stairs to the loft they would use as husband and wife until their own house was built in the yard.

Elimelek's heart was beating hard. He was glad no one had persisted in trailing after them for he wanted to be alone with Naomi when he lifted her veil, but now he was almost afraid to uncover her face. The last time he saw her, she had sprung at him, her fingers tearing at his face and neck.

Slowly he raised the veil. Her face, framed by the white scarf, was beautiful. She was smiling.

"Oh, Naomi, how beautiful you are. "

He pulled her to him and kissed her. He loosened her long braids, burying his face in her hair. He kissed her again and held her tight.

"Elimelek, I can't breathe! Elimelek, please . . . I want to tell you . . ."

He wouldn't listen, keeping his arms wrapped tightly around her.

Finally, she held him away. "Please! Please let me say this . . ."

She held his palms against her cheeks. "As God has proven that He hears the prayers of orphans and has given me you, my love, I promise . . ."

He pulled her back into his arms.

" . . . I promise to give you many children," she finished breathlessly.

Loud pounding on the door and calls from the yard brought them back to reality. "Elimelek, we want to see the bride! Bring her out! We're waiting to begin the wedding feast!"

The bridegroom kissed his wife once more. "Come, beloved." Picking up the fallen scarf, he draped it around her disheveled hair, and led her down the stairs to their wedding meal.

A time she dreaded was now upon Naomi: meeting Elimelek's family. These were the people she would spend the rest of her life with. What would they think of her? Naomi was determined to be watchful of her words and actions as she followed her husband across the yard.

The family was already seated in a circle around the food-laden mats. Naomi's spirits soared. How splendidly everyone was attired! Then came a nagging thought. Were they wearing their best clothes to show up her poor ones?

But she dismissed the thought when she saw the seven grandchildren. How precious they were! Their dark eyes flashed with exuberant health. For the moment they were sitting quietly, evidently under strict orders from the mothers, and watching the bride with lively interest.

Malkah rose and embraced Naomi, gently drawing her into the circle. "Come, Naomi, meet your new brothers and sisters, nieces and nephews."

Naomi nodded shyly when Malkah introduced the women: Aviah, Rahav, Zilpah. The three were petite and pretty, and the amount of gold coins attached to their jeweled crowns impressed Naomi. But she held her head high as she fingered her gold bracelets.

Elimelek and his brothers bore a great resemblance to each other. All had the direct gaze of men of freedom and action. In their bearded, handsome faces and sinewy bodies were strength and fearlessness.

Between them, dressed in white mantle and turban, sat the patriarch, Natan. He beckoned the bride to her place.

Timidly, Naomi held back.

"Naomi," Malkah whispered, "My husband signals you to sit beside Elimelek."

Naomi whispered back pleadingly, "I'm not accustomed to sit at table with men."

Malkah caught Natan's eye, and he understood. To cover Naomi's embarrassment he announced, "Let us lift our cups of wine and rejoice in the marriage of Elimelek to Naomi, daughter of our brave and noble kinsman Jashuv and his courageous wife, Merav. May the clans of Hamul and Hezron be united in glory in the sons of Naomi."

His respectful praise broke down Naomi's guard. Natan's acclaim revived her pride in herself. Tears ran down her face. She forgot she was going to hold herself in check and ran to her father-in-law and kissed the hem of his robe. The three daughters-in-law gasped. A hush fell. Naomi's exhibition of emotion was so spontaneous, so unexplainable.

Natan said kindly, "Naomi, my daughter, tonight your rightful place is beside your husband."

When she was seated next to Elimelek, Natan recited his usual blessing for bread and for freedom from slavery. Then the feasting began: bowls of honeyed dates and figs and grapes had been artfully spaced between baskets of freshly baked bread and spiced cakes. Slender pitchers held pomegranate wine, grape wine, and date wine. On beds of shiny dark leaves lay heaps of tender heads of lettuce, pungent green onions, cucumbers, and olives. Apricots, oranges, and melons added color and fragrance to the food-filled mats.

Many toasts were given and much wine drunk before Naomi realized the wives were saying nothing. She wondered at their aloofness. Then it dawned on her: they were offended at her behavior. She had acted like a slave-girl currying favor from the master by kneeling and kissing his garment. Proud Hebrew women did not kneel except in prayer.

Naomi hung her head. She was overwhelmed by her own effrontery in touching Natan's robe. She wished she could run away.

With prompting from the grandchildren, Natan said to his sons, "Mattityahu, Shmuel, we are ready for the meat."

The two men went to the fire-pit and returned with a whole roasted lamb on a spit, which they set before Natan and Elimelek. The children clapped their hands in delight.

Looking up, Naomi saw the luscious roast, and it brought to mind a conversation she had had with her mother when she was a child. "I love meat!" she had said. "I never have enough!" To which Merav had replied, "Little one, when you grow up and get married you will have all the meat you can eat at your wedding." The remembrance brought a smile to her lips that Gerash, one of the young grandsons, saw.

In his high-pitched voice he asked, "Naomi, at your house, did you always get lots of meat? We never do, except at festival times and I never get enough!"

The childish complaint was so exactly like hers that Naomi burst into laughter. All eyes turned to her, and in answer to their questioning looks she told them of her conversation with her mother.

Now all the children urged:

"Tell us more about what you did when you were little."

"Do you have brothers and sisters and cousins like us?"

"Did you have a lamb of your own like I do?" lisped a little grand-daughter.

"Do you have enough meat now?" asked Gerash, gorging himself happily.

Naomi blossomed under the children's attention, forgetting her recent distraction. Her quick responses to the children's questions sparkled with humor. She added remembrances from her childhood that she had never told anyone. Natan and his sons were surprised. The girl had charm! Even more, she was intelligent. Elimelek felt proud.

Naomi herself could scarcely believe she was talking so glibly. For five years her speech had been curt to everyone but Elimelek. What had loosened her tongue now?

Malkah said, "We are glad we have fulfilled the promise Merav made to you. I knew your fine mother and father, Naomi."

"My new parents have given me bountiful wedding honors. I offer my thanks."

Malkah thought, *What a pleasing personality she has. I like her forthrightness.* Aloud she said, "I regret that Elimelek and you must leave before dawn. But on your return we will talk at great length and become good friends."

Soon the three sisters-in-law carried the stuffed and sleepy littlest ones off to bed, the older children dutifully following. None of the three had addressed a word to Naomi.

Her joy dimmed again. She understood their coolness, and she wanted to crawl to the women and beg their pardon for her thoughtlessness. She knew what havoc jealously played among the women sharing a household.

"Naomi, why don't you eat?"

Startled out of her unhappy reflections, Naomi looked at her husband. There was concern in his eyes for her and the regard in his face exalted her: she was his wife, with the same privilege to sit in this family circle as the other wives. She raised her head, straightened her shoulders, and smiled. She picked up her bowl of food and ate hungrily.

Out of his house ran Gerash, the mischievous one. As he threw his little arms around Naomi, he knocked the bowl out of her hands and kissed her. The men laughed and Naomi's joy overflowed as she hugged him.

From the doorway his mother called, "Gerash, kissing the bride will not save you from going to bed. It is way past the hour. Come quickly!"

"Aviah is right," agreed Natan. "It is way past the hour for Elimelek and Naomi, too. Since they will leave early, I will give them my benediction now."

Everyone rose. Elimelek brought Naomi to stand before his father. In priestly fashion Natan laid his hands on their bowed heads.

"My children, Elimelek and Naomi, heed my words of blessing and instruction: May God who is the great shepherd of all, men as well as herds, keep you from want and suffering. May He lead you toward green pastures, and to quiet-running waters . . ."

The benediction was lengthy, but every word filled Naomi's heart with love and peace. When he finished, Natan embraced his son and his son's wife.

As the couple started toward the house, Malkah stayed them. Taking Naomi's hand in hers, she said, "Already I feel you will be as dear a daughter to me as Elimelek has been a son. I want to add my blessing to my husband's: May you soon become a mother."

Then she added, "For your journey we have loaded three donkeys with all you will need. I know you will be a capable manager for Elimelek."

Naomi bent down and kissed her new mother. Malkah felt the wetness on Naomi's cheeks and no more words were needed between them.

They parted, with Malkah returning to the wedding feast, and Naomi following Elimelek. Before entering the house, Naomi looked back at the circle of people around the fire.

I have become a member of this family by marrying Elimelek, she thought. *Now I want to be loved and welcomed here for myself.*

Before dawn the next morning Elimelek led his herd through the sleeping streets to the gates. He had to waken the watchmen and help them slide the weighty bars of cedar wood out of their slots, then laboriously swing open the thick cypress doors. The gatemen waited until the shepherd, his herd, and lastly, his wife were out, then slowly pushed shut the gates, each one creaking in its stone socket.

Naomi ran to catch up to her husband. She surprised him with the suddenness of her arms around him, her eager kiss on his lips. He was quick to return the caress, and with his arms still around her, asked, "Do you see those high hills over there?"

She nodded.

"They will be our home until the rains. Would you like a mountain for your home?"

"I gladly accept your mountain as my home. The green pastures will be our beds, the clouds our soft covers, and the trees our discreet friends!"

Elimelek smiled. He had hoped it would be like this.

They followed the moving herd arm-in-arm. Leading them was Tak, the ram whose large head with its crinkly, graceful horns was visible to all the ewes and lambs.

"We'll try to make the first stop when the sun is high by the big rocks," Elimelek said. "We can wait out the midday heat by a small spring there. In the cool hours, we'll resume walking and perhaps reach the caves before dark. We'll find sheepfolds there for the night."

"What will I do to help?"

"How about helping Tak in seeing that the herd doesn't nibble the green shoots in the cultivated fields," Elimelek teased. "As my father says, 'Keep them on the righteous path.'"

"You know Tak doesn't need my help."

"Well then, what do you want to do?"

"Let me go ahead and prepare the noon meal."

Now Elimelek laughed. "What will you prepare for me, O my zealous housewife? In all the marches I have made alone and managed to survive, what will you prepare for me that I can't take out of the baskets myself?"

"Oh, Elimelek, please! I want to see what your mother packed."

"All right, if that will make you happy. Take the two asses that carry baskets. The one with the fodder goes along just to carry back the skins of any sheep who may die. Mind you, walk the asses slowly."

"If I walk them slowly," she answered saucily, "you will get to the spring before me."

She pulled the two donkeys out of the line of march. As they progressed through the fertile valley, the countryside woke up. Barnyard animals grunted, cattle lowed, farm women called to their sleeping children. The swish-swish of field knives against ripe, dry grain filled the air like a rhythmical chant. It was the beginning of a new day in the homeland of the Israelites.

At first the sun warmed Naomi's head and shoulders gently, but in an hour, the rays were hot on her face. She looked back and saw that she had not gained much distance over her husband.

"Come on, walk faster! Oh, I forgot to ask Elimelek your names. Please walk faster, what's-your-names!" she urged the asses.

The sun was almost overhead when she reached her destination. Just as Elimelek had foretold, a brook ran along grassy banks surrounded by huge boulders. Naomi tethered the little donkeys close to the water to drink their fill.

Carefully she opened the many bags and baskets. She found sealed jars filled with oil for cooking and for lamp lighting, and special oil for medication. Large leather bags contained a mortar and pestle and kernels of barley and wheat. Other bags held dried fruit and fresh vegetables. A small pouch bulged with salt. Two goatskins held milk and water. In bundles tied with goat-hair rope was everything needed to shelter them, plus two long coats made of sewn sheepskins.

This is all ours! marveled Naomi. *I'll make the food last a long time. I'll stretch it by looking for wild berries, nuts, flower seeds, even wild honey. I'll show Elimelek what a fine provider I can be.*

She had to make haste. First she drew water and filled natural runnels carved in cup-like grooves in the boulders. Then she set out the noon meal.

When Elimelek approached, she ran to meet him and they kissed as though long separated. "Naomi," he said, "I would have married you sooner had I known what my herd and I were missing!"

When the meal was over, she asked, "Shall we start soon?"

Elimelek squinted at the cloudless sky, the burning sun. "I see that I'll have to start your first lesson right now on how to be a shepherd's wife," he said. "Sheep are like children: would you take them walking in this sun with no shade from glare and heat?"

Naomi shook her head, "But you said that we should reach the caves by nightfall."

"No, my wife, I said that if we could, we would try to get to the caves by nightfall. But when there is enough grazing, I let the sheep eat and move at their pleasure. The caves are more distant than they seem from here. If we don't reach them by dark, we'll sleep in the open field."

"Oh."

He couldn't resist teasing:, "Wouldn't you like to sleep under the stars, with the soft clouds for your cover?"

"That isn't what I meant," she answered. "I was thinking of the beasts of the field."

"What about them?"

"In my childhood, sitting before the night fire in front of our farmhouse, I listened to neighbors and visitors tell stories of beasts of the field attacking sheep and men alike. I dared not ask questions and call attention to myself, or I would be sent off to bed. But many nights I had terrifying dreams of being torn alive by wild animals."

"Beasts of the field are mostly mountain wilderness animals," Elimelek said. "As long as we keep a fire burning we have nothing to fear from them. Tomorrow I will whittle a heavy rod and a hooked staff for you and show you how to use them. With those weapons, you won't have to worry about being eaten alive. Come along, I'll introduce you to your charges."

He rose and pulled her up by the hand. Together they examined the sheep, who were standing with their heads tucked against each others' side for shade. The littlest lambs stood inside the shadows created by the larger animals. The shepherd called each one by name and showed Naomi how to recognize them.

"Tak! Show your mistress what a fighter you are!"

Tak lowered his head, his horns pointing menacingly at Naomi. Alarmed, she stepped back. Elimelek laughed.

"Don't ever be afraid of Tak, my darling. As long as he is king among the females, he is gentle. If the ewes get unmanageable and blunder about, as females are apt to do . . ." The lovers grinned at each other. "Just get Tak to order them into line again," Elimelek finished.

Tired from the enervating heat, husband and wife sat down in the shade of the boulders. With Elimelek's head on her lap, Naomi kept watch while he slept. A few hours later he awakened, and calling Tak to take the lead, they started out again. Before sunset Elimelek halted the march. They were still some hours' walk to the caves and night would fall swiftly.

"Naomi, unload the poles and ropes. You're going to make your first sheepfold. I'll stake out the area and pound the poles into spaced intervals. You'll tie the ropes, fence like, to the poles and as Tak leads the sheep in take an accurate count of them."

She did as he directed and gave a sigh of relief when all of the sheep following Tak into the improvised fold were accounted for and the herd safely gathered for the night.

Naomi set about preparing the evening meal by first digging a shallow pit. She filled it with brush, laid smooth, flat stones over the brush, and skillfully set it ablaze by twirling a piece of flinty rock against the stones. Her oven was now heating.

She pounded some wheat into flour and mixed in salt and water to make a batter of unleavened dough. After she flattened it into thin, round cakes, she laid them on the hot stones: when one side was browned, she turned them over to bake on the other side. The smell of bread baking made Elimelek's mouth water. Naomi spread a mat and set milk, vegetables, and fruit on it.

"Bread is ready!"

The call brought Elimelek quickly to table.

They sat opposite each other, and Naomi waited for her husband to help himself. But he sat, hands folded in his lap, drinking in the entire scene. Behind his wife was the large sheepfold, representing the wealth of the family. In front of her was the food she had prepared. Everything around Naomi symbolized the fruitfulness of the female: the capacity to provide, to produce, to create.

"Take off your shawl," he said. "Loosen your hair."

She untied the head covering and shook her braids until her hair cascaded around her shoulders. The firelight caught the glow of her eyes and hair, illuminating her face.

"Eternal One," Elimelek said, "I thank You for the abundance of our food, for the riches of our herd, and for this woman!"

Naomi was shocked. "Elimelek! Men don't thank God for women!"

"I say thanks for mine." They ate together in companionable silence, and when Elimelek said he was tired, Naomi discovered that she, too, was feeling the effects of the long march.

"Where do we sleep?"

"Here."

"Here? In the open? But, I'm cold. Don't you think we ought to put up the tent?"

"Put up the tent for one night? Oh, no."

He stood up, stretched, then searched through the bundles. He came back carrying the two coats, two mats, and his rod. "I'll build the fire to last the night through, Naomi. We'll sleep close to the herd."

He cleared stones and large pebbles away from the built-up fire, then spread the sleeping mats on the smoothed-out space. When Naomi slipped on the furry coat, it enveloped her from shoulders to toes—a marvelously warm bed. Tying her shawl firmly around her head, she lay down beside her husband, who was adjusting the rod within reach of his hand. Elimelek pulled Naomi close against him and she had never felt so safe, so warm, so protected. She fell asleep immediately.

Something woke her. With her eyes still closed, she thought, *I can hear Elimelek's even breathing and the sounds of the sheep in their sleep. Why am I awake?*

She opened her eyes: she was lying on her back, looking straight up at the bright, friendly stars. She moved . . . now she knew what woke her. Across her right arm, which was flung toward the dying fire, was something so heavy she could feel its weight pressing her arm down into the sharp points of small pebbles.

She was frozen with fear and could not bring herself to turn her head to see what lay on her arm. She thought, *If Elimelek, who sleeps with his senses always alerted to danger is not aroused, then I have nothing to fear.* But, still, she wouldn't look.

She debated whether to waken Elimelek and decided not to. After all, if they were in danger, wouldn't they know? Wouldn't they feel it?

After what seemed an eternity, when her arm was completely numb, a cinder dropped into the fire with a sputter. Instantly, the thing rasped itself across her arm and rustled into the brush.

The moment it moved, Naomi knew it was a snake. She lay there, wet with nervous perspiration. *You have saved me, God of my ancestors and my parents,* she prayed. *You have saved me from the bite of a serpent!*

She couldn't raise her paralyzed arm. She forced her fingers to curl shut and open until they felt shot through with stinging barbs. She bit her lips to stifle her groans. As she rubbed the arm, blood began to course through it normally. She turned on her side so as not to awaken her husband, and drawing the revived arm close to her body, she fell asleep again.

"Wake up, sleepyhead! It's time to go." Elimelek was shaking her gently.

Naomi awoke with a start. It was dawn. The sheepfold was gone, the asses were loaded, the fire extinguished, and the herd moving ahead.

"Why didn't you wake me? I should have done the packing."

With a smile, he said, "Some things I can still do, my wife, before you make me entirely helpless."

Naomi jumped up, slipped off the coat, and rolled it up with the mat. She hurried after him and Tak.

They were now so far beyond the region of fertile farms that Elimelek could relax his vigilance in keeping the herd on the right path and let them scatter out and eat whatever they could find. Ahead were the green Judean hills, and the sheep scampered eagerly to the slopes.

Elimelek thought it was time for another sheepherding lesson. "Do you know what makes a successful shepherd?" he asked Naomi.

"Having a helpful wife?" she teased.

He grinned. "Well, yes, now that you mention it. What else?"

"Not walking your sheep in the heat of the day," said Naomi, repeating what Elimelek had taught her earlier.

Elimelek nodded. "Good shepherds also watch the horizon for sudden rain clouds in order to find shelter before the sheep get wet feet—drenched feet mean sheep rot, which usually ends in death; they probe the low trees and bushes for lurking beasts; they are aware that a sudden drop in temperature forecasts a blizzard—a sudden rise means a wind and sand storm; they keep special watch that the smaller and weaker lambs don't fall behind and become prey to hawks and eagles; they use the hooked staff to help the clumsiest sheep out of ruts or traps—they can easily break their legs falling in; they watch out for . . ."

Naomi was only half-listening. Her mind kept drifting back to her close encounter with death the night before.

By noon they reached the foot of the hill. The open caverns in the limestone rock were elevated above the floor of the valley. They made excellent sheepfolds because they were cool, dry, airy enclosures.

Nearby a small waterfall trickled down the side of the hill. It fed a minute oasis: acacia trees with feathery foliage, bushes and grass still green, all surrounded by a brown sea of sun-dried land.

"This is a Garden of Eden," Naomi observed.

Elimelek agreed. "But only until the water dries up and the grass is gone." What he didn't say was: "Or until the other shepherds come this way and fight me for the water and the grass." Why should he worry his wife?

Naomi set out the meal in front of the cave while Elimelek unloaded the donkeys. With an instinctive knowledge never to tell a man questionable news when he is hungry, she waited until the meal was over, then told him about the serpent.

His reaction was unexpected. "Naomi, never be so foolhardy again! The snake is a stealthy beast. With his poisoned tongue he brings death to livestock and people alike. Had you nudged me, even slightly, I would have killed him swiftly with my rod. You let him get away to do damage elsewhere."

"But I hated to disturb your sleep," she said. "You needed your rest."

"Do you think I'm incapable of protecting you and the herd if I don't get enough sleep? Have I not said that shepherds must always be on guard?"

Naomi tried to withdraw into herself, to feel untouched by Elimelek's scolding, but love made her vulnerable: she burst into tears.

"Don't cry, dearest. I didn't mean to be harsh," he said as he held her closely. "Please try to understand the danger all of us were in. I don't know why the snake didn't bite you. Maybe it had just eaten its fill of field mice and was satisfied. I can only say that God was watching over you."

Naomi quickly wiped her tears away and silently gave thanks to God for protecting her beloved Elimelek. She plunged into work. "We can have butter and cheese with our bread tonight," she said after she asked Elimelek to make a tripod for her.

Elimelek cut down three sturdy branches. By tying them at angles to each other, he fashioned a tripod from which he suspended the goatskin Naomi had filled with milk. After the milk stayed in the skin for a while, it turned sour; by rocking it, she knew that the sour milk would eventually become butter. Naomi emptied half the butter into a bowl, reclosed the skin, and continued to rock the buttery contents so it would thicken into clotted cheese.

There she sat, contentedly rocking the goatskin in front of the cave that would serve as sheepfold for the sheep and a temporary home for her and Elimelek. The heat of the sun was subsiding, a fresh cool breeze stirred the leaves of the trees, and within earshot was her loved one, tending his herd. She was filled with peace and happiness again.

She tried to sing as she worked. *Well, this isn't singing,* she thought. *It's more like the croaking of a frog.*

"Elimelek," she called, "will you teach me how to make music?"

"Very well, beloved, as soon as I'm done here."

He was anointing the scratches and bruises of some sheep. Pouring oil from a ram's horn into the sore spots, he rubbed the wounds. When he finished, he went into the spring and pulled up some hollow reeds. Breaking one into the required size, he punched five holes into it with a sharp twig.

"Here's your flute. I'll hold it to your lips while you blow."

She blew as Elimelek rapidly ran his fingers over the holes. Naomi was delighted to hear the trill of different musical tones.

"You shake the butter," she said. "Let me play the pipe myself."

Elimelek rocked the bag and Naomi blew into the reed. In a short time, the sounds became clear and sweet. Tak nosed up, a quizzical look on his long face, followed by some ewes.

"Stop it, Naomi," laughed Elimelek, "or you will have the herd crowding here thinking it is time to have Tak lead them into the cave."

Naomi tucked the flute into her belt. The gurgling sounds in the skin had ceased and the heavy mass at the bottom was solid cheese. She dumped the contents into a bowl and began to make bread. As she cradled the mortar bowl in one arm, she pounded barley kernels with the pestle to make flour. All the while, she watched the little sheep running up and down the side of the hill. How carefree they seemed! One found a rocky ledge to stand on. Others bleated as they came up to him and tried to push him off. They were funny, like children.

Impulsively she set down the flour mill and pulled off her head shawl. *I want to jump, too!*

Hindered by the long dress, she drew up her skirt-front high into her belt to free her legs and thighs. She ran to the hillside and with the goats and kids, jumped from rock to rock.

"Who . . . eeeeee . . . who . . . eeeee," she shrilled in flight. The breeze lifted her unbounded hair like a waving banner. The warm wind caressed her thighs and the exhilaration of the moment affected her like heady wine. She ran higher and higher up the hillside, jumping from jutting rocks without fear.

Elimelek smiled at her enjoyment. Suddenly, a few feet above Naomi, a shadow moved. Elimelek's eyes held the spot as he withdrew a slingshot from his belt, crouched down to pick up some stones, and fitted them into the sling.

Naomi was singing the notes of the flute, poised for another leap when she saw her husband advance on her. The notes died in her throat. Minutes before he was smiling at her. Now his eyes were hard, the smile gone. He was coming straight at her with the whirling slingshot in his right hand, his rod readied in his left hand.

She stood still, wide-eyed, frightened.

Making no sound, Elimelek twirled the shot faster and faster, and when he was almost up to her, he raised his hand and shot the stone above her head.

Naomi screamed and fell off the boulder she had been standing on. Elimelek spurted behind the boulder, where he clubbed a stunned jackal to death.

Naomi sat where she fell, rubbing her skinned knees and arms.

When Elimelek returned to her, she burst out, "You terrified me when you came at me! I thought you were going to kill me!"

He smiled, then became serious. "This proves how vigilant we always have to be. Your life, and the herd's, is always in danger."

Naomi felt that she had failed her husband a second time. She watched him dig a hole and bury the jackal, then said, "Show me how to guard against these beasts."

"All right, we'll start with the shot because you'll use it many times. If a sheep or goat runs away, shoot a stone in front of it; that will stop it. Shoot at any shadow that moves. Do it like this . . ."

She studied his movements, then nested the pebble, twirled the sling, and shot with all her might. The stone hit the face of the boulder and bounced back. She picked it up, tried again, and the same thing happened.

"I can't do it . . . it won't go over."

"Watch me."

With exaggeratedly slow movements he demonstrated how to use the slingshot as a lethal weapon.

"Practice it, and when you've mastered it, I'll show you how to use the rod and the staff."

Naomi spun and shot, retrieved the pebble that fell short, spun and shot again until her arms and shoulders ached. But she did not give up until she achieved three successful shots.

That night, while she counted the sheep into the cavern sheepfold, Elimelek built up the campfire outside. They lay down to sleep in the entranceway, their bodies making a human gate.

What good were my promises to do more for Elimelek than another wife? Naomi thought. *I have yet to prove my worth.*

"Elimelek, the summer is almost half over, and we haven't seen another shepherd in all this time."

"I planned it that way," Elimelek answered. "Why would I need anyone's company when I have everything I want in you."

It was true: Naomi's every act was calculated for her husband's safety and well-being. She rose before him in the morning and fell asleep at night only after he and the herd were quiet. Her senses were now as Elimelek's, attuned to the beautiful yet hostile world around them.

Soon Naomi had killed her first fox, and her husband remarked on her skill with the rod and the slingshot. But she was hungry for more of her husband's praise.

"Did I do as well helping fat Tovel out of that hole?"

"Yes," said Elimelek, "Tovel would have broken her legs trying to scramble out if you had not given her a well-executed lift with the staff."

"And will you trust me to doctor the sheep as you do?"

"You know I trust you. I've seen you prepare medicine-soaked sticks, scour out worm-infested wounds with no hurt to the sheep, and doctor the wound before the animal knows what you're about. Soon you'll be teaching me new skills!"

As Elimelek led the herd to ever higher pastures, Naomi felt awed by the grandeur of Judah's hills and fascinated by the strange flowers, birds, and animals living there. Looking down from a lofty pasture to the valley far below, she asked, "Are you sure we can't see God from these high places? Surely He must be close to us here."

Elimelek quietly replied, "He is close to us everywhere."

How long they remained in any one place was unpredictable. They might pitch their goatskin tent for weeks in a good field, then in a matter of hours, move it to another slope. Every twilight they built a fire to last the night through, and if they heard sounds of prowling animals close by, husband and wife picked up burning torches and circled the herd, counting and checking.

One very dark night on such an inspection tour, Elimelek heard Naomi cry out in terror from the other side of the fold.

"Come quickly!"

In the light of the flickering torches, a few yards from where Naomi stood, lay Tovel's mangled, half-eaten body. Straddling it, eyes glaring and fangs dripping blood, panted a lioness. She was a gaunt, yellow beast whose emaciated ribs swelled up and down over her bloated stomach. She was still ravenously hungry, and her low-throated growl was an ominous sound.

Elimelek pushed Naomi back.

"Hand me another lighted torch," he commanded softly, "then get far behind me. This beast is so desperate she will fight me rather than give up the kill."

Naomi's hand shook as she put a second brand in Elimelek's hand. In the wavering light, her husband looked pitifully frail against the elongated, looming body of the lioness. Naomi trembled. She wanted to, but could not, close her eyes to shut out the scene: the man digging his heels down to make firm his footing while slowly raising the firebrands, and the lioness stretching back down to the haunches, her legs readied to spring, her hanging tongue salivating out of her open mouth, fangs bared.

The second she vaulted, Elimelek hurled the torches with deadly aim into the lioness's face and eyes. The burned and blinded animal screamed.

Elimelek waited until the thrashing lioness ceased leaping, and coming from behind, he clubbed her to death.

Naomi's stomach turned queasy and she ran. Her fear for her husband and the sight of the gory death brought on a severe attach of nausea. Unseen by her husband, she fell to the ground, retching, then lay sick and trembling. Her torch smoldered and went out.

The cautious shepherd was searching for the pride of lions. He called out a warning, "Naomi, these animals travel in families. If the king lion ate first, he will bring the rest here. Guard your side of the fold and if you see anything, shout!"

She couldn't answer; she was too sick to make a sound.

After a while she heard him say, quite close to her, "Naomi, why did you let your torch die out? Speak, so I'll know where you are."

He almost stumbled over her. "Naomi, what happened? Are you hurt? Were you attacked?"

He picked her up and carried her to the campfire.

Naomi put her arms around his neck. "I wasn't attacked. I have never been so frightened in my life. If your torches hadn't found their mark, I . . . I would have wanted the beast to kill me, too."

"But you've seen me fight wild animals to the death before, and you were never sick this way."

He felt her forehead, her cheeks. "You don't have a fever. You are usually so unafraid, so courageous that it's hard for me to believe that . . . Oh! Naomi! How many months have we been married?"

"It will be three months with the new moon."

"Naomi, you're going to have a child!"

She stared at him. Of course! She had been so anxious for it to happen, yet so unsure. Now Elimelek had said it, and it must be true.

Incredibly she felt fine. She sat up and laughed. Elimelek laughed at her laughter, and in the stillness of the night their laughter echoed from hillside to hillside.

The next morning Naomi gathered the remnants of the dead sheep's skin. "Poor Tovel," she said to Elimelek as she tied the scraps to the donkey's back. "She was such a good friend, so kind to her babies and us. And now we've lost her."

"Be glad you have those pieces of her hide left," was her husband's matter-of-fact reply. "Had the lioness dragged Tovel's remains off to her cubs, we would have nothing to take back to Bethlehem. And we need to show that we didn't sell such a valuable ewe."

"Oh! Are these few pieces enough to show that it was Tovel who was killed?"

"They're enough."

"But what will your family say when we tell them we lost her?" Naomi asked. "Isn't it your responsibility to show an increase in the herd?"

"As long as I can show proof that I didn't sell Tovel for my own profit," Elimelek said, "I won't have to pay the family for the loss."

By now the sheep had grown large. Underneath their dirty, oily gray outer wool coats, their fleece was thick and creamy white, their skins pink and unblemished. As Elimelek was quick to admit, it was Naomi's doctoring that kept the animals in peak health, her watchfulness that kept the herd intact.

For a few months they encamped near the top of a ridge. One night Elimelek announced, "Tomorrow we leave for the valley on the other side."

"I hope we'll find wheat and barley fields there."

"We will."

"I'm glad. We're low on grain."

Elimelek then explained that he had waited for a reason. "The valley is a table plateau between high hills. It has cultivated fields, good grazing, and water holes. It's known to all the Bedouins. By waiting until when I think they've left for their desert homes, I've avoided having to fight them for grass and water. But we can't wait any longer. The grass and water here are almost gone."

"Don't worry about Bedouins, my dearest. You have me to help you. I'll fight by your side."

Her innocent bravado touched Elimelek's heart. He gripped her to him, as if to prevent losing her. "I don't think you'll be called on to fight, my warrior-wife," he said. What he refrained from telling her was that the wandering desert robbers stole women as well as sheep. Elimelek had seen many such captive women tied to caravans and dragged back to desert strongholds, while their husbands lay murdered in some clump of bushes or lonely cave.

The plateau was like a table spread with nature's bounty. Naomi saw fields ready for harvesting, orchards laden with fruit, and clear-running streams. She bartered her goat's cheese and butter for grain and fruit and vegetables from the farmers.

Husband and wife erected their tent not far from a water hole surrounded by low trees and leafy bushes with plenty of grass around. The next day while the two were engrossed in their labors, they heard a loud clap of thunder. They scanned the sky. Not a cloud was there.

A little while later they heard another clap. This time Elimelek took a quick count of the herd. Seizing his weapons, he called, "Naomi! Get your rod and knife! Come with me!"

She did so, running with him into the thicket of bushes.

"Keep your head down!" he warned. "And be quiet!"

"Why?" she whispered, "What is it? What are we doing here?"

"Look!"

Elimelek parted some of the underbrush to create a small opening. On the other side of the water hole Tak was in a violent battle with another ram. The stranger-ram had huge ringed horns with ridges sharp as knives. When the two ran head-on into each other, the impact sounded like thunder.

"Stop them! Tak will be killed!" Naomi scrambled to get out.

Her husband pulled her back. "Hush! Don't make a noise. The ram

Tak is fighting must belong to Bedouins who haven't left this area. They may be as close as just beyond the farmhouses."

"Bedouins? I thought they were gone!"

"I had hoped they were."

"What should we do?"

"Stay here under cover."

Elimelek drew Naomi into his arms. "Dearest," he said, "promise me this: if we are surrounded, stay in here. I will go out alone. They may never suspect you are here. And if something happens to me, I will wait for you in the land beyond, in Sheol."

She pulled away from him. "No! We'll attack together, take them by surprise, and fight side by side. When I am with you, I fear no one. Alone, I would die anyway."

They sat in each other's arms, watching the battle between the rams and waiting for the Bedouins who would surely appear, attracted by the thunderous noise of pounding hooves and resounding head crashes.

"Why are they fighting in such a meaningless way?" Naomi whispered. "They paw the ground and dash at full speed to butt their heads together. Then they disentangle their horns and do it all over again."

"One ram has to be the victor," Elimelek explained, "whether he kills or just wears out the other."

"But why? Why can't there be two rams in a herd?"

"It's their nature. Only one male can rule, no matter how many females are in the herd."

"Oh! The other ram has made Tak bleed! I told you it might happen if you didn't stop them!"

"Don't worry about a little blood," Elimelek answered. "Tak is experienced and can take care of himself."

The shadows of the rams lengthened as the hours wore on. Husband and wife remained hidden, watching, waiting. Finally the stranger-ram pawed the ground without vigor, his body weaving as he ran. Exhausted, he dropped at Tak's feet. Tak waited, then shook his head as if to clear it, and walked away.

"Tak won't be bothered any more," Elimelek said, "but I can't understand why no one has appeared in all this time. Stay here until I call you."

He crawled out of the hiding place and looked around. "Come here!"

he called. "I want to show you something!" When she stood beside him, he said, "We're in luck! That ram is wild and Tak has just tamed him for us. There are no Bedouins here."

"Are you sure about the ram?"

"See his open wounds? Bedouins take care of their livestock. They would have cured those injuries. He's a beauty and he'll obey Tak, so there won't be any more fighting."

Naomi examined the prostrate ram. "Oh, Elimelek, may I have him? For my own?"

"Your own? Why?"

"I'll bring him back to health and he'll be ours, the first of our own herd." She stroked the newly tamed animal. "And I know what I'll call him. His name will be Yod, *the hand of God.*"

The weather suddenly turned hot and dry and the early rains did not come as expected. Elimelek knew that they would need to travel much further than expected in order to find the fertile pastures for the sheep. It was over two more months before he and Naomi could finally dismantle their tent and set out homeward.

During these months, Naomi's body slowly changed as the baby grew inside her. On the march home, Naomi gazed down at her protruding belly and said to her husband, "I have such mixed feelings about going home. I'm sad to give up having you all to myself, but I'm happy that our child will be born where grandparents and relatives will be there." To herself, she admitted that the child would give her the social standing she had been wanting.

The journey home was uneventful and short. They only took time for overnight rest and sufficient grazing. At last, late one afternoon, they sighted the well outside Bethlehem.

"I've unpacked clean changes of clothing," Naomi said to her husband. "We'll wash and change before we go into the city."

Elimelek looked at her with surprise. "Why? It's not the Sabbath. Everyone knows what shepherds look like after the long march."

"Please, my darling, do as I ask. It will make me proud if your family can say how fine you look since you married, so healthy and well cared for."

Elimelek indulged his wife. While the herd drank at the well, deserted at this late hour, husband and wife washed and changed clothes. "Do you know," Elimelek said, "this is the first time I'm returning with only one dead sheep's skin? All the other years, the third donkey's back has been piled with losses!"

Naomi smiled: she knew she had proved her worth. Whistling to Tak, she and Elimelek took the familiar path to the city's main highway.

"The roads are as empty of people as the night I fell in love with you," said Elimelek. "But, somehow, it's a different emptiness. I don't hear birds singing. Even the hoot of the night-owl is missing."

They looked up into the sky. Hawks and vultures were flying in lazy, quiet circles. There were so many of them. And there was such a dreadful stillness on the road leading to the gates. Apprehension quickened their steps.

A ghastly sight soon met their eyes. The huge wooden gates were ajar with dead bodies blocking the entrance; men hung lifeless over the walls. In the marketplace the dead were lying strewn about, some headless, some burnt in pyres, some partially consumed by wild beasts and scavenging birds. The stench rose in their faces.

Horror-stricken, Naomi turned to her husband.

"The Amalekites!" he said.

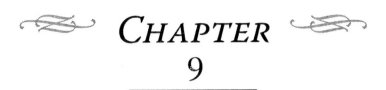

CHAPTER
9

Alarmed by the foul odors, the sheep baaed loudly, backing away in confusion.

"Quick, Naomi! Get the herd home as fast as you can. Don't stop for anything on the way. Use your rod if anyone tries to stop you!"

"Where are you going? Aren't you coming with us?" Naomi's voice was high-pitched with panic.

"Remember the cave where I saw you the first time? Once before, my family had to hide there. I'm going to see if anyone is left alive."

His wife stood irresolute, bewildered.

Elimelek gave the ram a smart slap, commanding, "Tak, take them all home!" and the next moment he was running out of the gates.

Naomi pulled the shawl over her nose and mouth. With her heart beating fast, she followed the sheep in Tak's wake. The goats ran ahead, but the sheep were nervous. The first in line stumbled over the dead and hurt their legs; the ones behind tried to climb over the fallen and slipped off. Those in the rear ran blindly against the rough stone walls, scraping their sides.

Running back and forth, calling the animals by name, Naomi tried to calm them with her voice. She fought to control herself from screaming at the stupid creatures. Despite her anger, she managed to keep them together.

As they bumbled along, she had to shut her eyes often to blot out the sight of the animals' hooves stepping on the dead, spattering pools of blood. The streets were the same as the marketplace. Death and its stench pervaded everything.

There was no need to fear anyone stopping them. Not a soul was alive to hinder their way. She reached Natan's yard, and even as she called, "Father! Mother!" she knew that no one would answer. Her voice had only its echo for answers.

She remembered to count the herd as they walked into the pen and was thankful they were all there. She looked into the homes with their doors hanging awry. She saw broken furniture, shattered tools, and smashed storage jars with the precious grain strewn and despoiled with oil. She examined everything more closely: there was no blood. Everyone must have been taken into slavery!

Darkness was descending rapidly. She unloaded the asses and found two little saucer-shaped lamps. She filled them with oil from her own supply, lit them, and sat down to wait.

Eternal One, please let Elimelek find someone. Please let there be someone alive!

Finally, she heard a rattling at the gate. "Elimelek!" And then she saw her parents-in-law. "Father! Mother! You're safe!"

She helped her husband guide his weary, unkempt parents into the house. She removed their shoes and gently washed their streaked faces and hands. "Don't move. I'll prepare milk and bread," she told them.

While Elimelek helped his father eat, Naomi steadied the bowl of food for her mother-in-law. Malkah smiled wanly, "My daughter, you are like a ship that brings food from afar. You are so good, so kind."

Naomi wanted to cry but made herself smile comfortingly at her parents-in-law. It was not easy to hide her heartbreak at the sight of Malkah's haggardness and Natan's torn clothes and matted hair. She whispered to her husband, "Father stares like a child."

"I see it too. Something must have happened to his head. He doesn't seem to comprehend what we say."

Natan finished first. Scraping the bowl, he said, "My, that was so good. My son, my daughter, God heard my prayers and kept you from returning while the Amalekites troubled us. They are gone and you are safe. Now all will be well again." He smiled happily.

"Father, I want you to rest, but . . . just one question. Where are my brothers?"

"Didn't you see them? They must be somewhere on the fortifications above the gates. They were among the first to man the walls," Natan answered proudly.

Elimelek turned to his mother. "Where are the women, the children?"

Malkah's eyes in her drawn face were stoical. "In slavery," she told

Elimelek. "We survived because our sons were able to get a few of the elders, their wives, and us out of the city before the barbarians struck. The younger women fought by the side of their men."

"What happened?"

"It was five days ago. Your father called a meeting of the council. He had repeatedly warned them of the need to unite the tribes, but it was already too late. The raiders were on the way. They came so swiftly that there was time only to barricade the gates. There was no way to seek help.

"For two days after they stormed the gates, we heard the screams from the murderers and the murdered alike." Involuntarily, Malkah covered her ears.

"Mother, say no more. Wait until you feel stronger to tell us."

She shook her head. "I want to tell you now and never again speak of it."

"If you wish . . ."

"On the third day, finally, there was silence. Soon afterward, from our hiding place we saw our sheep, goats, and oxen tied in pairs and driven off with the rest of the plunder. Last of all, our fields were set on fire."

"The crops gone? That means starvation!" Naomi said.

"Worse yet, most horrible to witness, our women and children were sold into slavery and tied by the necks in long lines to Midianite caravans. I saw little ones stumble and get kicked to death by animals' hooves. This is when your father got hurt."

"How?" asked Elimelek.

"He could stand no more of the brutalities he saw. We tried to hold him back, lest we all be discovered, but he ran out, knife in hand, and struck at a tall, burly slave-master. That man was so strong that he just shook your father off, then beat his head with a rock. He left him for dead. When the caravan was gone, we crept out and rescued him." She stroked her husband's cheek.

Elimelek was forced to look away. His face burned with anger as he tried to imagine the horror that had taken place. Naomi lowered her head and wept silently.

"Please rest now," Elimelek said to his parents. "Tomorrow we will make plans."

Up in the loft, Naomi and Elimelek lay in each other's arms. "What will you do now?" she whispered.

"My father's mind is gone. My heart hurts that I should take his authority from him, but I have to assume charge immediately. Clearing and planting have to be done first. Perhaps those elders who survived and are strong enough will be willing to help me."

"Elimelek, does any one have livestock in Bethlehem?"

"You heard what mother said . . . not an animal is left."

She waited.

"Naomi! I have the only livestock in the city. I cannot let anyone near. Those people will kill our herd for food!"

"I know. We have to keep the knowledge of our sheep from them, but you have me to help you clear and plant."

"You're big with child. How can you bend to dig and plant?"

"Don't worry. I'm strong and the child within me will be no hindrance. The two of us will accomplish more than the elders could."

The next morning Elimelek said, "Father, you must promise that you will not tell your friends about our herd."

"I promise. Just tell me what to do."

Natan tried his best to be of help but after one morning's effort, he grew tired and wandered away, seeking his old friends. Elimelek, Naomi, and Malkah labored in secrecy. They repaired the sheepfold, and contrived a sturdy lock on the inside of the yard-gate. They took the sheep out at night for pasturage, when the old people were asleep.

It was not difficult to hide their work from the elders, who were overwhelmed with the task of cleaning the marketplace and streets. They needed help burying the dead. Natan tried to be of service but he was undependable.

"Bring Elimelek here," they said. "He's young and strong."

"Elimelek can't come."

"Why not? What selfish task is he doing that he can't serve his community?"

"I can't tell you."

"God was kind to Elimelek and saved him from the massacre. Has he become a heathen that he shows no gratitude?"

Natan resented the insult to his son's character. "You can't speak of him like that. He's anointing the injured sheep!"

The men dropped their work. "What sheep?"

They turned from Natan to consult in low tones. Disturbed by their side-glances and whisperings, Natan hurried home and locked the gate as he was cautioned to do, but the frenzied mob of elders were close on his heels. When they tried to enter, they called over the waist-high stone fence, "Natan, unlock the gate. Let us in. We want to talk to Elimelek."

"I can't do that. Elimelek is busy."

"Dear friend Natan, please let us in to help Elimelek. If we could but work for him, perhaps he would pay us with a little milk or cheese."

The old patriarch stood alone in the yard, gazing with tears in his eyes at the friends of his youth. Their skinny, aged hands extended to him in supplication, and their cries were more than he could bear. Compassion overruled his clouded mind and he unlocked the gate. The men surged in, shoving Natan aside in their rush to fling open the door of the pen and lay their grasping hands on the sheep.

Naomi, alone near the door, was bent over a sick sheep, medicine-soaked stick in hand. She was painfully tired after hours of guarding the sheep at night and working in the fields during the day. The babe within her was restless and squirming. Suddenly, she was surrounded by men dragging sheep out the door.

"Elimelek!" she shouted above the excited baaing of the sheep and the braying of the asses. She ran to bar the door so no one could leave. "Elimelek! Quick! The door!"

"Out of our way, woman!" barked an old man.

As Naomi stretched her arms wide to block the passage, the old man struck her on the head with the back of hand, knocking her through the door to the ground outside. As he stepped over her, he dragged along a resisting sheep, followed by the others doing the same.

Naomi attempted to stand up but her body was so unwieldy she fell to her knees. In frenzied haste, she stayed on her knees and waddled until she caught the first man's legs and held them so tightly to her that he fell headlong, yelping. Naomi's action gave Elimelek time to reach the gate and bar it with his body.

With a rod in one hand and a staff in the other, he looked at the crowd of elders with angry eyes. "Take your hands off my sheep!" he commanded. "If any of you dares to take one, I will kill him!"

The old men feigned surprise and grief. "Natan!" they called. "Come listen to your son! Is this the respect we get from him? We who are the elders of Bethlehem's council? Shame on you!"

Natan approached Elimelek. "My son, what harm is there if these men take a few sheep? They are hungry and it is God's law that we share with the needy."

Without lowering his weapons, the young man replied, "Father, your friends are stealing not a few but many of our herd. We cannot feed this mob and survive ourselves. I must choose between feeding them and feeding my unborn child. I choose to feed my child."

Natan, who could only agree, nodded. Turning to the elders, he said with childlike sincerity, "My son is right. You and I have lived our lives and served our purposes. We must leave food for the children. Please go home in peace."

But hunger made the men reckless. They thrust Natan against the wall and attacked Elimelek with rocks and stones, fists and feet. Down came his rod and staff while he tried to beat aside hands, heads, and bodies.

The attackers grew more vicious. They threw sand and larger rocks into the young man's face. He grew winded and his arms ached from holding so many at bay. Blood that flowed from cuts on his forehead ran into his eyes and blinded him. His strength was ebbing when suddenly Naomi was by his side, striking blow after blow at those who tried to get past them.

The elders fell back. They had not expected to deal with this formidable opponent, despite her clumsy body. Naomi bristled with righteous indignation and newfound strength. She swung her weapons with both hands.

Now it was the old men who tired. They backed off, one by one.

Elimelek issued orders: "Move away from those sheep! Father! Mother! Get the herd back into the sheepfold."

Not until this was done did Elimelek and Naomi stand aside. The bruised and resentful elders limped out of the yard, empty-handed.

The two warriors embraced each other.

"You saved me, Naomi! I could not have held out against them!"

"No, my love, it was you and our child who saved us. I never would have had the courage to strike the elders. But when you said you chose to fight for our child's life, I was no longer hindered by my awe of them."

She held his swollen face in her hands and wiped away the blood. "I would have come to your aid sooner but I was having difficulty over . . ."

"Over what?"

"Myself! I couldn't get on my feet. Every time I lifted myself to my knees, someone in back would hit me, and down I would roll like a ripe apple."

Elimelek roared with laughter. She *was* round like an apple.

That night, up in the loft, Elimelek warned, "What happened today is only the beginning. The men will come again."

"What will we do?"

"Double our efforts. On wet days Mother and Father will keep the sheep locked in the fold. On dry days we'll all go to the fields so we can start planting immediately. The rains are still light, and the ground is sufficiently soft. The sheep can graze near us."

"But how will we plow without heavy tools and oxen?"

"We have no alternative but to use ourselves. I'm hoping you'll be strong enough to steady a makeshift plow while I pull it."

"Of course I will be strong enough. I promised, didn't I, that I would never fail you, especially now when you need . . . oh!"

A convulsive shudder shook her. "Ohhh . . ."

"What is it? What's the matter?"

"My back! I have such pains in my back! Please wake Mother. I don't know what . . . Oh!" she screamed.

Thoroughly alarmed, Elimelek woke his mother. "It's Naomi. Something is wrong!"

Malkah rose quickly, took one look at the heaving, writhing girl and said calmly, "Nothing is wrong. It will be all right. Go, my son, I'll call you when it's over. It seems that your child is coming earlier than expected and Naomi fights now with the evil demons determined to kill him. Go, wake your father and leave this house or you'll be defiled by contact with the demons."

Elimelek was relieved and comforted: his mother was a woman who could face demons and win battles. She would bring his child safely into this world.

Between body-wracking spasms, Naomi and Malkah talked.

"You are having a son," Malkah observed.

"How do you know it will be a boy? My mother had only a daughter."

"Don't doubt it will be a boy. I know."

Naomi looked up into the face bending over hers. *I don't think I could have loved my own mother more than I love her. I want to be like her . . . if I live.*

She closed her eyes with a grimace of pain. Beads of sweat rolled down her face and neck. She bit her knuckles to keep from crying aloud.

Malkah grasped Naomi's hands. "Take hold, squeeze my hands tightly, and scream out against the unholy spirits who are preventing your son from coming," she instructed.

Naomi gripped the work-hardened hands. "Yes, Mother, I will scream and I will fight. I fought people who hated me, I fought thieving beasts, I fought the council elders, and I can fight evil spirits, too. The demons won't touch this child. I will prevent them, even if I die for it . . ."

She ranted on and on until at last Malkah put her hand over the girl's mouth. "Enough, Naomi. Your son is here," and Naomi fell into exhausted sleep.

Immediately Malkah picked up the infant by the legs, slapped him on the back once . . . twice. The baby's mouth relaxed, a thin wail came out. Malkah cleaned him carefully with salt, wrapped him in swaddling clothes, and laid him in the straw-filled manger.

Then she attended Naomi, cleansing her and covering her warmly. Gently she combed Naomi's perspiration-wet hair into neat braids, and last of all, tidied the room.

She opened the door. "Elimelek, you have a son."

"A son! I have a son! Oh, Mother, you knew it would be a boy!" He kissed her joyously, then embraced his father. "What will we call him?"

Natan furrowed his brow, pleased to help. "I remember! If I had had another son, I would have called him Mahlon."

"Mahlon? It's a fine name, a worthy name. Mother, may I go in now to Naomi?"

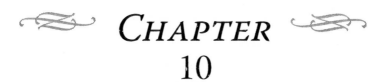

After one day of rest Naomi got up from her bed, bursting with happiness. As her infant nursed at her breast, renewed vigor flowed through her. She laughed aloud when she heard Elimelek call from the gate, "Naomi, can you hurry our son? He's already late to work. His grandfather and grandmother have long since taken the herd to pasture."

"Here we come now," she sang. Motherhood had brought instant changes to Naomi. Her sharp, bold features were now softened by a tenderness.

Elimelek peeked at the baby asleep in the wool cradle slung across his mother's back. "Mahlon, my little son," he marveled as he drew a gentle finger over the baby's downy hair.

He handed Naomi a filled water skin to carry, then swung a crude plow over his shoulder. It was fashioned from a wooden stake, sharp-tipped at the bottom, handles at the top and ropes threaded through slots in the shaft.

When they reached the scorched fields he said, "You hold the plow and I'll put on the harness."

Naomi shortened her dress into her belt, so that her legs were free of the encumbering skirt. As she pushed down on the plow handles, Elimelek pulled, and slowly a shallow row was furrowed in the warm, moist earth. For hours they worked, and whenever Naomi raised her eyes, she saw her husband's perspiration-covered back, glistening in the sun.

Naomi's mind began to wander. *In all the world there's no one so handsome, so strong, so capable as he is.*

A moment later, Mahlon's cry interrupted her thoughts.

"Stop, Elimelek, I want to see what ails him."

Elimelek threw off the harness. Naomi dropped the plow, and bending forward, she swung the cradle from back to front. Tiny, wrinkled Mahlon was gnawing his pink fists between cries.

"Ho, my hungry little man, time already for another meal?" Sitting down in the furrow, Naomi opened her dress and nursed the child.

Elimelek stretched out beside them to rest his aching back. Lying prone brought on a fit of coughing, and he had to sit up. "I must be getting old," he said as he rubbed his chest. "I haven't pulled a plow in so long, I'm stiff and full of pains."

His wife looked at him sympathetically but her mind was on other things. "I've been thinking about Uncle Hepher and his family. Do you think God punished them because they were unkind to me?"

"Misfortunes are not necessarily punishments for wrongdoing. God's ways are hard to understand. Why should my brothers and their families have been killed? They never harmed anyone. Perhaps there's a deeper reason. Don't you think your own suffering made you a courageous woman? I do. And I think that's why I fell in love with you."

He rubbed his chest again and changed the subject. "I may have to reorganize our labors. I'm afraid I can't pull the plow fast enough to get much done. I may have to take the asses that Father and Mother are using to haul dung. Well, let's try one more row."

Mahlon had nursed his fill and was fast asleep. The parents' rest time was over. Once more Elimelek harnessed himself to the plow. Naomi gripped the handles and pushed. Head down, hands and shoulders straining, her eyes on the overturning earth, she began to see glints of something in the dirt beneath her feet. Red, gold, green, blue—she kicked at the objects in the furrow.

"Elimelek, wait!"

He turned to see his wife on her knees, scooping up handfuls of dirt. "What is it? What are you doing?"

"Look!"

In her hands were jeweled crowns, hung with gold coins: Malkah's, Rahav's, Aviah's, and Zilpah's wedding crowns!

Elimelek fell to his knees and dug the earth, too, uncovering brooches, amulets, earrings, rings, chains, and bracelets. "My brothers must have buried these right after they left Father and Mother in the cave."

"What should we do with them?"

"Hold Mahlon in your arms and carry the jewels in the cradle. Go home and bury them. Oh, and Naomi, never speak of them to Father or anyone. Someday, we'll need them."

Naomi hesitated. "Don't you want me to help you finish the plowing first?"

"No, go now. You've done more than enough good for today." He kissed her. "Bury the jewels deep and mark the spot."

Holding the swaddled Mahlon closely, Naomi hurried through the field to the city where the roads were filled with people. When the news of Bethlehem's ravagement had reached the other tribes, belated aid came. Kinsmen and friends arrived with cattle, grain, and provisions. Others came to claim or buy property. Usually Naomi was glad to see newcomers fill the city, but not this morning when she felt all eyes were on the bulging cradle on her back.

That night, Elimelek asked, "Where did you hide the jewels?"

"I dug a deep hole in back of the sheepfold and buried the jewels right in the wool cradle. I made a mark with pitch on the wall above. Believe me, I want to forget they are there."

In spite of the austerity of the times, when Mahlon was eight days old, his parents invited the important townspeople to their home to celebrate his circumcision. Elimelek performed the religious rite with a polished stone knife while Natan, holding the child in his arms, intoned the solemn words: "Blessed be he who comes to swell the tribe on his eighth day. As an abiding symbol that the children of Abraham are consecrated to the Lord of Abraham, we cut the flesh of the foreskin of this man-child, for cleanliness is sacred. In his blood he has life: in the marks we have made on him, he is initiated into God's covenant with Abraham. May his hands and heart be firm with love for God."

It was a happy celebration and during the feasting Natan blessed Elimelek and Naomi and sang of the future greatness of his grandson. Naomi's heart overflowed with love for everyone, especially her father-in-law.

Seven months later, Natan closed his eyes in sleep, never to awaken. Lovingly, without tears, Malkah prepared her husband for his final journey. With Elimelek's help, she dressed Natan in his luxurious white mantle and kissed his closed eyes in farewell. She placed the high turban on his head, so that he appeared in death as he did in life—dignified and patriarchal.

Following the bier to the burial cave walked a silently weeping Elimelek, a self-contained Malkah, and an inconsolable Naomi, who was again with child.

Malkah worried about her daughter-in-law. "Your grief is drying your milk," she warned Naomi. "Mahlon won't be able to get enough nourishment from your breasts. You must not cry after Father."

Through her tears Naomi gazed wonderingly at her small mother-in-law. *How brave she is. The mainstay of her life is gone, but her concern is that the living should be strong for the future. If anything ever happens to Elimelek, I pray I will be like her.*

After her second son, Chilion, was born, Naomi arose from the childbed more anxious than ever to be at Elimelek's side. He was working beyond his strength. Although the city was swollen with itinerant workers, soldiers, freed slaves, and beggars who formerly looked for work, they now refused hire. Greedily they tried to get rich by fighting for unclaimed property.

Many nights Naomi woke up to find her overtired husband pacing the floor and rubbing his chest and arms where the pains were the fiercest. She wept inwardly. *If only someone would come to help. If only his brothers were alive. I'm afraid for Elimelek and I'm afraid for Malkah. Both are laboring beyond their strength.* And she fought her own exhaustion to make the work lighter for the others.

Naomi was sheepherding on a hillside with her attention divided between her little sons rolling about on a blanket, the herd nibbling grass, and her husband and mother-in-law laying seed into the plowed land below.

From where she stood, Naomi could also see the distant highway, on which a strung-out caravan of donkeys had come to a halt. As she watched, a young woman stepped down and ran to Malkah, arms outstretched. The old woman put down the bag of seeds and fell into the stranger's arms. Elimelek, too, dropped his bag and clasped both women in his embrace. Naomi could tell they were all crying. A tall man who followed after the woman also fell into their arms.

Naomi's heart beat fast. *It must be! Elimelek's sister Yocheved and her husband have come home!*

She saw Elimelek cup his hands around his mouth and shout some thing up to her. She waved and watched as Malkah ran to the caravan where children, still seated, waited. At the same time, the two men and the woman started up the hill toward her.

Yocheved was as tall and slender as her brother. Naomi thought her sister-in-law carried herself with an assurance that must have come from years of making her own decisions, away from parents and brothers. But when Yocheved kissed Elimelek's cheek and laughed at something he said, she displayed a girlishness that showed she was still the adored sister of his childhood.

Chilion wailed. Naomi picked him up and patted his back until the moment when Yocheved stood before them. Naomi saw such warmth in her sister-in-law's deep brown eyes that she felt a heavy load lift from her heart. Yocheved held out her hands for Chilion and wordlessly Naomi put the baby in them. With that gesture, she gave her love and trust into her new sister's keeping.

Yocheved kissed the baby. "I have come home, Naomi, too late to bid Father farewell, but in time to greet the newest Hezronite." She introduced her husband. "This handsome man is my Hanoch."

Naomi turned to Yocheved's lanky, craggy-faced husband. He appeared much older than his wife until he smiled, and suddenly he was as young and as warm-natured as she was. Although tall, he seemed stooped from years of leading caravans into the wind. His large nose was crooked, perhaps broken in fights with thieves. Yet he was all gentleness as he smiled his greeting to Naomi and picked up the crawling Mahlon.

Malkah came hurrying. "Naomi! Elimelek! See my beautiful grandchildren!" She pulled them along with her, three stalwart boys and three vivacious girls. Malkah was crying and kissing the little ones, the middle ones, the grown ones. It was a family reunion that she had not dreamed possible.

That night, after the meal, Yocheved said, "When we heard that Bethlehem had been ravaged, I asked Hanoch if we could go home. I felt sure that some of you must be alive and would need us. So Hanoch sold my bazaar and all the merchandise we had on hand. We used our caravan to transport our household here."

Amazed, Elimelek turned to his brother-in-law. "You spent years building your reputations as honest, reliable merchants. And you gave up your trade and Yocheved's profitable shop to come to Bethlehem?"

Hanoch looked at his wife with unabashed love. "Yocheved wanted to be here."

The next morning Elimelek and Hanoch said to the boys, "We'll divide the tasks of sheepherding and farming between us. The women can stay home."

From that day on, life was joyous for Naomi. With the help of Yocheved and her daughters—Sara, Bracha, and Yehudit—the household chores were lightened and there was time to talk and relax. She was surrounded by love and approval, and she gave of herself to her nieces, nephews, and their parents unstintingly. This was her family dream come true.

But, in a few months, Malkah found it difficult to rise from her bed. She called all the children and grandchildren to her. With effort she said, "My loved ones, God has seen fit to bless me in my latter days with more abundance than I deserve. I feel that soon He will call me to Sheol and I am eager to go. Natan is waiting for me. My daughters, Yocheved and Naomi, my only sorrow is that I have no inheritance, no family heirlooms to leave you, nothing for you who are so dear to me—"

"Mother!" Elimelek interrupted. "I had forgotten! You do have your jewels. We found them more than a year ago, hidden in our field. We will bring them to you."

The treasure was dug up, and in Malkah's presence the men, wives, and children cleaned the dirt-encrusted pieces. Once more the crowns, gems, and gold pieces shone brilliantly.

Malkah smiled drowsily when she saw them. She closed her eyes, dreaming of the past when these precious ornaments meant much to her and her three dead daughters-in-law.

Suddenly she opened her eyes wide. "Naomi! Yocheved! You must do this right now. I wish to see you divide everything between you!"

And they all watched as the two women took equal portions of the inheritance. Then Malkah closed her eyes and sighed contentedly. Her wish to provide had been fulfilled.

In the years that followed, Elimelek and Hanoch, Naomi and Yocheved, together with the children, worked gainfully and harmoniously. Their herds increased and their farmlands abounded with produce.

On only one subject did the women have divergent opinions. Yocheved loved people and it was her habit on the Sabbath to meet with her friends Nechama and Tova. They would stroll to the marketplace or to the well and acquaint themselves with the women new to Bethlehem. Naomi would not accompany them because she preferred to rest on the rooftop or watch the children at play.

"Naomi, you must come with us today," Yocheved said. "Please don't refuse. We met such an interesting woman last Sabbath, and we are all eager to see her again."

"Thank you, no. I don't need to meet any women. All the female company I ever desire is right here in our house."

"If you won't come, I will bring her here. Listen to me, Naomi, not all women are like the ones you knew in your uncle's house. There are women in the city who can add beauty to your life, if you will only meet them halfway."

"I think not."

That very Sabbath Yocheved brought home Kezia, a newcomer from Jericho. She was a quick-moving, thin woman with piercing eyes who was the same age as Naomi. She would have been pretty had she allowed herself some adornment, but she was severely plain despite her expensive dress. Kezia's nose tilted upward, giving her an air of disapproval. When she walked into the house, she glanced sharply into the corners. She greeted Naomi with, "I cannot abide waste or filth. I am comfortable only with people who have sensibilities like mine."

Naomi wondered if Kezia ever listened to her own voice. High-pitched and shrill, it reminded Naomi of the women in Hepher's household. The voice grated on Naomi's ears.

Yocheved picked up an unfinished conversation. "Kezia, you were telling me that you have been traveling in the territory of Dan. Were you and your husband visiting relatives there?"

"My husband was not traveling with me. I went alone with his oldest son and a guard."

"Alone?"

"Yes, of course. I always travel with one of his sons and a guard."

Intrigued, Naomi asked, "Always travel? Where? I've never heard of a woman traveling . . . just traveling."

Kezia selected a bunch of grapes from a tray, examined them closely, and said between nibbles, "I've traveled to so many places I can't remember them all. I travel for my husband to buy land. When we hear of someone wanting to sell property, I go first to see how much it's worth. If it's worthless I tell my husband so, and he is spared the journey. He has bought and sold many very good properties."

"Does he always trust your judgment in these matters?" Naomi had to ask.

"What do you mean trust me? If I say buy, he buys. If I say no, he doesn't. Why do you suppose we are rich? Not because of him! He dawdles at home."

Naomi was astounded: a woman who commanded her husband. Now there were two reasons she didn't like Kezia: her voice and her personality.

Kezia saw the shock in Naomi's eyes. She smiled. "Any woman who has greater ability than her husband should use it to his advantage. It's no disgrace to him or to me that I'm wise in the ways of trading and he isn't. Since men will not deal with me, my husband carries out the decisions I make. I'm no fool like his other wives. He married me because he knew I could do more for him than those cackling hens."

Naomi was stunned. Could Kezia be speaking the truth? In Naomi's experience, men were all-wise, all-knowing. That a woman could do better, or know more, was unheard of.

Kezia did not hesitate for words. "Let me tell you something else, Naomi. I am given to quick judgments and I am never wrong. Without knowing either of you, I have already judged you: Yocheved will make her way peacefully and successfully in this world because of her natural goodness. But, you: you, Naomi, are a different kind of woman. You are my kind, a fighter. I can tell by the way you talk and look at me."

You are mistaken, thought Naomi. *I look at you with distaste.*

"I will make you a gift, Naomi. I like to teach, and if you wish, I will teach you a great deal about other cities, other peoples, their customs, fashions, cosmetics, inventions, and many more things that I have seen and learned."

"You could? You would?" Naomi said excitedly. She was surprised to hear herself saying these words to someone whom she barely knew .

But Kezia had said magical words that offered to open mysterious doors for Naomi.

"But why, Kezia? Why would you want to give your time to me, a stranger?"

"Let me put it this way. I will find it enjoyable to share the long, idle Sabbath days with you, while escaping from the company of those chattering idiots my husband has for wives."

She glanced out the door and noted the lengthening shadows. "I must go now," she said as she rose, "but look for me next Sabbath."

"Yocheved, that woman leaves me breathless!" Naomi said when Kezia had left. "I don't know what to make of her."

Yocheved confided that she had once asked Nechama and Tova about Kezia. "They said the key to her personality lies in her husband. He is a handsome, lazy, arrogant man who had many mothers in his father's house. They vied with each other to grant his every wish, and now his wives do the same. Kezia is the wisest. She keeps him bound to her because he is greedy for the money she shows him how to make. If she is an aggressive woman, it is jealousy of the other wives that makes her so. Three of them are younger and prettier than she is."

"Oh."

"Naomi, you may never like her, but you will benefit by what she teaches you, and in time, you may even come to admire her."

As it turned out, Kezia enriched Naomi's life in many ways: from the tales of places Kezia had visited by ship and by overland travel, to the knowledge she imparted of how other people lived. She taught Naomi how to make dyes from powders imported from Babylonia; these produced colors more beautiful than the old dyes that came from berry juices, roots, nuts, and beetles. The result was that never before had Naomi's clothes been so richly hued, so becoming.

Kezia had lived in Egypt for a few years and learned there the art of making perfume and cosmetics. She taught Naomi how to concoct salves and ointments and how to apply cosmetics and perfumes to her face and body. Naomi lost no time preening herself for Elimelek, who was enchanted with her new allurement. He became more attentive and Naomi was ecstatic with the effect she had on her husband.

A year later Kezia left on a journey of several months. As the months passed without Kezia's companionship and instruction, Naomi came to a realization.

"Yocheved," she admitted, "you were right when you predicted I would one day come to admire Kezia. I never believed I would miss a woman friend as much as I miss her."

"I'm glad to hear you say it, because I've noticed lately how silent you are, and I wondered what was making you unhappy. Is it Kezia you have on your mind?"

Naomi sat with downcast eyes. "Yes . . . I miss her."

Yocheved persisted. "I think it's something else. Naomi, you have everything you want: husband, children, family, friends, wealth. But you're not yourself."

"It's nothing, no more than what's troubling everyone in Bethlehem these days."

There was great apprehension in the city. The time of the early rains had arrived weeks before, and not a drop had fallen. The earth was parched, seared by the relentless sun. Prayers for rain were chanted, precious cattle sacrificed, to no avail. Pasturage for the herds was gone from the hillsides, the wells and streams mere trickles, no wind stirred the air.

Although she was filled with foreboding of an oncoming drought, Naomi often wept in secret for another reason. *Why am I not with child?* she wondered. *Why, when I want a baby so much?*

Already her sons were little men. Mahlon was eight years old, as serious and industrious as his father. Chilion, in his seventh year, was still short and roly-poly. Naomi found his ways adorable, but when she tried to hug him, he wriggled out of her embrace.

She recalled with longing the time before each of her sons was three years old. On each boy's third birthday, a great feast was given in his honor. The occasion was his weaning: he was no longer dependent on his mother's breast for nourishment. Each time, Elimelek and Hanoch made speeches extolling the boy's manliness. And that was the last time Naomi was able to hold her sons close and feel that she alone provided all they needed.

When they were five years old, Elimelek took charge of their education. He taught them to fish, to catch game in nets and snares, and to labor by his side among the herds and in the fields.

After a long day of work, little Chilion dragged his feet, weary beyond words, but he never complained. Naomi ached to lift the fatigued child in her arms to comfort him. But the other boys would tease him, so she stifled her yearnings.

The men in the family interrupted Naomi's recollections.

"Get food and water ready for us," they said.

"Where are you going?"

"There is nothing we can do here, so we will take the boys partridge hunting."

"Chilion, too?" asked Naomi.

"Of course."

The women and girls filled scrip bags with food and leather skins with water, while the men readied bows, arrows, and nets. The group marched through the gate with Chilion last, struggling to hold on to all his equipment.

Watching him, Naomi's control burst its bonds: impulsively, she ran to his aid, then snatched him up to kiss him. He ducked his curly head and reproached her with his large, brown eyes. "Don't, Mother! I don't like that!"

Elimelek turned around. "Naomi," he chided, "have you forgotten that you weaned him four years ago? He's a man now. He goes hunting for food."

Naomi ran into the house crying. Yocheved followed. She put her arms around the weeping woman and said, "We're alone now, Naomi. Tell me why you are so sad."

Naomi hesitated. "I've done a terrible wrong," she whispered. "In desperation last winter, without Elimelek's knowledge, I went to the old women in the Canaanite village. I had prayed for so many years for more sons, to no avail, so I bought the magical potion they make from mandrake roots, the potion that makes women fertile."

"Naomi!"

"It was so stupid of me. Not only was I in danger to venture into that abominable idol-worshipping hovel, but it's obvious the potion was worthless. Oh, Yocheved, I am an unfruitful wife, as barren as the soil of Bethlehem." Naomi wept.

Yocheved looked compassionately at the woman her brother loved. Naomi was like a flower in full bloom: petal-smooth skin, beautiful red lips, and lovely body. She was magnetic, and yet she was in despair.

"Yocheved, I don't know what to do. I give my love to Elimelek without reservation. I'm strong and healthy. Why can't I fulfill the law for wives?"

It was almost dark when the men and boys returned, empty-handed. That night, Hanoch, Elimelek, and the oldest sons sat in the gates with the men of the city. There was no talk, as in previous times, about uniting with other tribes and electing a king. Of greater concern was the fact that cattle lay dead in waterless streams, pastures were brown wastes, stinking fish marked dry watercourses. The partridge, gazelle, and bird-life had fled the naked hillsides, and the grain fields were stubble-covered deserts.

At last the elders rose to pronounce the decision of the council. "We are grieved to declare that Bethlehem is in a state of famine. Since there are no visible signs of relief from the scourge of drought, the people should wait no longer. They must quit their homes and the city!"

Cries of protest came from the most poverty-stricken: "Already we've placed ourselves in bondage to get food for our families. Will they be forced to go while we remain? What about our children seized by our creditors because we're unable to pay? Are we to desert our children?"

The elders shook their heads in sorrow. These were the added disasters the drought brought in its wake. Without water or food, the council was helpless to save anyone.

Each man had to resolve his problems in his own way. Those families with reserves could migrate immediately either to the north, where the green fields of the tribe of Dan were sheltered by the Lebanon forests and watered by the Upper Jordan River, or to the east, where the lofty table-land of Moab had received sufficient rainfall to keep the pasturelands alive.

The women listened stoically to the news the men brought home. Naomi said, "It doesn't matter to me where we go; my only wish is that we go together. I want to be with Yocheved and Hanoch. I want my sons to be raised with their cousins. I want us to continue living as one family, with one purse, and one home. If Natan and Malkah were alive, I'm sure this would be their wish too."

Yocheved nodded her agreement.

There was silence, then Hanoch spoke, his voice grave. "Naomi, dear sister, I know that for Yocheved's sake and the children's and mine, I should say, 'You are right. Come with us, back to our city in Dan. My home and land is there, and my kinsmen would welcome you.'"

Naomi wondered what he was about to say.

"It grieves me to tell you this, but for Elimelek's sake, I think you should go to Moab."

Naomi looked at her husband, questioningly.

Hanock appealed to his brother-in-law: "Forgive me for breaking your trust. I have labored for six years by your side. I have held you in my arms when the pains in your chest were unbearable. You asked me not to tell Naomi . . . I can no longer spare her. She knows of your illness at night, but not of the suffering you endure in the day. Because of it, I beg you to go to Moab where the air on its heights will be healthier for you than in the north with its extremes."

Naomi ran to her husband and buried her head in his chest. "Why didn't you tell me? How could you keep this from me?"

"Don't cry, Naomi, please. Perhaps Hanoch is right. The climate might help me. We'll go to Moab."

The next morning Elimelek and Hanoch divided the sheep, the food, and water supplies. The asses were loaded with everything of value, and the women hid their money and jewels inside their clothing.

Then the two families went to the burial cave to say a last farewell to Natan and Malkah. After that, Naomi went alone to the burial cave where her father, uncle, and aunt slept and took leave of them. When she returned home, Kezia was waiting.

Naomi smiled at her with joy and sadness. Her friend had come back, but now it was Naomi's turn to leave.

"Will I ever see you again?" her friend asked.

Naomi hugged her. "If God wills it, we will see each other again. I'll be lonely for you, but I understand why you remain—your husband's livelihood isn't dependent on herds and grain fields. I'll pray for our reunion to be soon."

"Here, Naomi," said Kezia, "take this scroll I've written out. When you reach Jericho, go to my kinspeople on this street. Give them the letter; it contains an order to shelter you in my house for as long as you wish. When you resume the journey, I have instructed them to give you food, supplies, and herbage for your sheep."

Naomi wept unashamedly.

When Kezia left, there was nothing to do, no need to wait. Already the streets were clogged with families streaming out of Bethlehem. At the gates, Naomi hugged her nephews, then held Sara, Bracha, and Yehudit close to her, kissing their cheeks, smoothing their hair.

But when she and Yocheved clung to each other, the tears flowed without restraint and speech was difficult. "I'll ask you, as Kezia asked me, if I'll ever see you again," Naomi wept.

Yocheved couldn't answer. They kissed and broke away when the men called impatiently.

Hanoch, Yocheved, and the children, with Tak leading their sheep, merged with the hundreds of Bethlehemites going to the north.

Elimelek, Naomi, Mahlon, and Chilion, with Yod at the head of their flock of sheep, headed eastward, to the Judean wilderness.

Where now . . . ? thought Naomi.

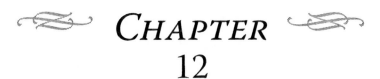

CHAPTER 12

For days they plodded through the rock-strewn hills and canyons that separated Judah from the Dead Sea. The scorched highways were ancient watercourses long dried out.

Elimelek tried to enliven the tedious journey for his small sons. "Within a few days you'll see a sight so wondrous you'll be the envy of your friends when you meet them."

"When, Father, when? How much farther do we have to go?"

Naomi was unhappy with Elimelek's choice of routes. To safeguard their possessions was insufficient compensation for traveling unaccompanied through the forbidding mountains.

The cheerless aspect of the arid gorges was dismaying in broad daylight: at night the loneliness was terrifying. The parents built a fire and took turns guarding the sleeping children and the herd. Hungry beasts that roamed the fields howled and screeched close to them.

Days passed and Elimelek pointed out landmarks so the boys could see they were constantly descending, getting closer to Jericho, until the day they stood on the last ridge.

"There it is . . . the surprise!"

"Oh-h-h-h!"

It was an unforgettable sight. Flat in the midst of a long, narrow stretch of land lay the Dead Sea like an enormous spread of blue silken cloth. From their vantage point they could see birds flying high overhead, but no living thing stirred the waters. Moab's mountains guarded the other side.

"This place is called the Plain of Yeshimon," Elimelek explained. "It's empty and abandoned because the salt in the sea kills living things."

"It's more frightening than the wilderness," whispered Naomi to her husband. "Even the savage beasts don't seem to come here."

They scrambled down the stony slope and for the first time in days, walked on flat terrain as they headed north. Ahead of them extended the eerie emptiness of the Yeshimon Plain and the embedded Dead Sea. On their right towered the brooding Moabite cliffs with their grotesque red, yellow, and black walls. Naomi felt nature's hostility all around them.

Soon a new fear overcame her: her breathing became labored, her legs felt wooden, and she had to force herself to walk.

"Mother, I'm so sleepy. May I rest for awhile?" Chilion's eyes were heavy-lidded and his little head drooped.

"I'm tired, too," said Mahlon.

Naomi looked at her husband, walking like a man in a stupor as he rubbed his chest. The intense heat was sapping their vitality; none of them could move normally. She had a horrible vision of their lying dead, burned up on the Yeshimon Plain like the people in the story of Sodom and Gomorrah.

She had to do something to save her family. She sprinkled drops of their precious drinking water on cloths and wrapped them around the heads of the three. From her garments, she withdrew the crowns and golden trinkets. She put the crowns on their heads, hung the chains and amulets around their necks, and put the rings and bracelets on their hands. Then taking Elimelek's pipe, she played lilting tunes and danced with swaying motions before them.

Perked up by the wet cloths and jewels and happy music, the little boys clapped their hands. Elimelek, too, straightened up and smiled at his wife's antics.

"Stop your dancing, Naomi," he soon cautioned. "We are approaching a stretch of slime-pits I have been warned about. The land is pockmarked with them. They are so slippery that if one of our sheep were to slide in, we'd never be able to rescue it."

They put away the crowns and trinkets and proceeded slowly. Watching every step, they didn't raise their eyes until Elimelek called out, "You can look up now! Way up. There it is, Jericho!"

In the far distance they could see spraying heads of palm trees against the blue horizon. Naomi's spirits soared: soon they would be with Kezia's people, where fresh water, companionship, and rest awaited them.

"How green it looks even from this distance," she said.

"Jericho is known as the 'City of Palms,'" Elimelek told his sons. "Its fruit orchards, grain fields, flower gardens, and vineyards are blooming because the Jordan River nourishes them."

By the time they reached the roads that crisscrossed before Jericho's gates, they could see crowds of travelers from Bethlehem milling about.

And something was wrong.

"Those people can't be our friends from home," Naomi said. "They look so starved. Their cattle are but skin and bones. And why are they standing before the gates? Why don't they go in?"

"Look!" pointed her husband.

Up on the parapets of Jericho's fortified walls, armed soldiers waited with bows and arrows pointed directly at them.

Like the other travelers, Elimelek and his family stood out of the range of the arrows; they felt sickened by the reception Jericho was giving her fellow Judeans. Naomi threw Kezia's scroll into a saddlebag—she would have no use of it now.

"Elimelek, son of Natan!"

Elimelek turned. "Shimon, my friend! I almost didn't know you! What has happened to you?" Elimelek couldn't believe the shriveled man before him was the jolly fat farmer he had known since boyhood.

The aged man shook his head. "My troubles have piled years of sorrow on my head. My only son, his wife and son, and I had food and water enough to get to Moab. Large families traveled with us, and one night the father of many children tried to steal our food. My son fought him and the two men wounded each other mortally. There was nothing I could do but share our food with the dead man's children. Now it's all gone."

A boy and a woman hovered close to Shimon. They wore the same look of starvation: hollowed eyes, skeleton-looking bodies, flapping clothes.

"Here are my son's wife and my grandson," Shimon said. "Guni is eleven years old and such a smart boy for his age."

There was love and pride, but also grief, in the touch of the grandfather's hand as he stroked the child's hair. Elimelek nodded to Naomi: she reached into a bag and drew out a cake of pressed figs, some cheese, and dried olives that she handed Shimon. He held the cheese to Guni's mouth, and when the weak child sucked it, the mother snatched Naomi's hands and kissed them.

There was no choice now for the travelers but to keep moving, to walk the sun-baked miles to the Jordan River.

After a day of rest by the river, Elimelek seated Guni on top of a bundle-laden ass, and with Naomi and the boys pulling and guiding the sheep, they all crossed the Jordan at a shallow place.

When they stepped out on land occupied by the Hebrew-speaking farmers of Moab, they saw unguarded wells, unfenced fields, fruit and vegetable gardens—all an open invitation for settlement. They were overjoyed at the hospitality.

For a day they wandered the open country and enjoyed the new sights. Shimon pointed to a forbidding mountain. "See over there, that rugged peak? It's Mount Nebo, where Moses looked across the Jordan River and saw the land promised to the Israelites. He died on Mount Nebo and is buried there."

The travelers began to hear loud screams and sounds of fighting. Shimon observed, "Already there's trouble. The hungry Israelites have no money, no barter for grain and oil. They are harassing the farmers for food."

"I want to get away from here immediately," Elimelek said. "Shimon, will you come with us to the high plateau? It's for my health that we go there."

"I thank you, but no, Elimelek. I'm too old and worn to undertake the upward climb to Moab's cities. Don't worry about us, my good friend."

"I will give you some gold to buy food," Elimelek offered.

"May God bless you, Elimelek, for your kindness, but I'm not in need of money. My son's wife has jewelry concealed in her garments. For your generosity, my grandson and I will never forget you. We owe our lives to you."

While Shimon embraced Elimelek in farewell, little Guni threw his arms around the friends he had learned to love in just a few days. The mothers wept as they told each other goodbye.

Elimelek and his family and herd left the troubled farmlands and followed a well-traversed road along the Dead Sea that led into a narrow river gorge. Steep walls rose on either side of a restricted river. The gorge was a dark, damp wonderland of cool air, tropical trees, unusual flowers, and birds.

"Another Garden of Eden" was Naomi's surprised observation.

"What strange colors are here," said Mahlon, as he studied the streaked layers of rock that gave the canyon its bizarre appearance. The brilliant sun, filtering down, struck shafts of light against the walls and highlighted the zigzag road leading skyward.

"Father, let's stay here until you feel better. It's so lovely," said Mahlon, who watched butterflies winging by.

"No, son, I can't breathe closed in here. I want to get up into the light air. Come, let's not waste time."

They climbed the upward road while pausing often for Elimelek to rest. Naomi's heart was torn by her husband's gallant effort to hide his suffering. Dependable Mahlon pulled the ropes guiding the herd, and Chilion kept an eye on the laggards; Naomi's arm was around Elimelek.

When they reached the top, it was not long before Elimelek said, "I feel better already. This air is easy to breathe and I have no pain!"

The Moab highland was a vast, rolling country, totally lacking in trees. There was nothing to obstruct the view that stretched ahead as far as the eye could see. The red-colored soil was rich, judging by the flourishing grain fields. Fat sheep and goats and oxen grazed in green meadows.

"Oh, what a blessed land Moab is!" Naomi said. "As Hanoch said, you'll regain your health here. How far do we go now?"

"To the king's city, which is the heart of Moab, two days' walk."

Chilion was worried. "Are you sure the king will let us live in his city?"

"Oh, yes. He'll be cordial when he sees we have gold to buy a house and more sheep. To the credit of the king, it's known he breeds only the finest and reserves much land for sheepherding."

"Father, where will we get grain and fruit and everything else?"

"We'll barter our cheese and butter, wool and skins for the king's grain, salt, oil, and other foodstuffs."

The king's city was impressively fortified, with banners flying from every turret. Inside the gates the Judeans were directed to the official headquarters of the royal steward in charge of the king's trade. While Naomi and the boys waited, Elimelek was ushered into the important man's presence and in a short while returned, followed by a slave holding a tablet and stylus.

"We have been granted permission to live here," he said to Naomi. "This clerk will help me select sheep. You and the boys are free to visit the city and find us a house. I'll wait for you here."

Excitedly, Naomi and the boys roamed the marketplace, spellbound by the treasures in this cosmopolitan city. It was, as Kezia had described it long ago, highly civilized. The square by the gates was three times larger than Bethlehem's and the shops were crammed with unusual, imported merchandise.

The boys came upon a circus troupe and Naomi had to pull them away bodily from the performing bears. "We've been here too long already. Father is depending on us to find a house; when we live here, you'll have time to go to the circus."

How different these streets were from the streets at home: unlike the noisy, snarled congestion of Bethlehem's unpaved, crooked, narrow streets, these were wide and straight and stone-paved, so that traffic moved smoothly.

High fences of stone and wood with carved doors shut the houses from the view of passersby. But where the gates were open, Naomi and the boys peeked in to see lawns bordered with flowers, benches, and statues, and rippling water playing in fountains. How different they were from Bethlehem's yards.

Naomi thought of Kezia's sharp criticism of the cities owned by the Hebrews: "They are dirty and uncivilized! Naomi, you should compare them to the cities in Egypt, Moab, and Babylon. There you will see such cleanliness, such superb sculpture, homes with such graciousness as you never dreamed! It is beyond the understanding of our stiff-necked Hebrews to appreciate such culture! Our Hebrews are fools! They free their slaves while other countries make intelligent use of them." Naomi had to admit Kezia was right about the cleanliness and beauty of the Moabite city. Everything was orderly and well-kept; slaves worked everywhere. She and the boys stood in admiration of a house and garden where a slave scrubbed the mosaic tile walk that led from gate to house. When her task was finished, the slave woman rose painfully to her feet, and for a moment looked at the three by the gate.

Naomi looked fully into the slave's face. Deeply etched around the faded brown eyes and sad mouth was an elusive sweetness and warmth, a fleeting resemblance to her mother, Merav.

The slave's eyes caught hers: Naomi's hands reached out; she tried to call her mother's name but just then a woman came out of the house carrying a whip. "Nayda!" she screamed. "Why are you standing there? Must I be after you all the time?" Angrily she raised the whip and struck the slave.

Naomi gasped. She fled and dragged the boys after her. "Mother," protested Chilion, "why are we leaving? Mother, don't hold my hand so tight!"

She ran with them toward a huge forecourt where many people stood waiting. She heard instruments playing and sweet voices singing. Wiping her tears away, she looked around, then up. High on a magnificent ziggurat where he commanded all eyes to look up to him sat a gigantic idol, a gold Chemosh. A yawning hole gaped where his abdomen should have been, and in the hole a fire crackled.

Marble stairs led up to the Moabite god and to the sacrificial altar before him. Priestesses were scattering flowers on the idol and his altar: Chemosh was awaiting a sacrifice. At that moment, bells chimed and a hush fell on the worshippers. Cymbals clashed and the multitude fell on their knees. Black-frocked priests followed by white-robed children began to ascend the stairs, and as they climbed ever higher the singing swelled louder and louder.

"Look, Mother! The king! The children are going to see Moab's king!"

Mahlon and Chilion were excited by the impressive sight: hundreds of Moabites, the fanfare, the music, the pretty children, and the awesome size of the glittering idol.

Horrified, Naomi said, "We have to leave, quickly!"

She hurried them to the royal steward's building where Elimelek waited, business finished.

"Naomi, what is it? You look so white!"

"Elimelek, let's leave here. Right now, please!"

"Why? What happened? You can talk; the steward is gone."

Her eyes were stricken. "I saw the idol Chemosh, a fire burning in him. The priests were about to sacrifice a child on his altar!"

Fear drove Naomi to ask, "Suppose the Moabites don't like foreigners in their midst and they seize our sons for their sacrifice?"

"Only Chemosh's worshippers are privileged to give their children to him," said Elimelek. "We never need to be afraid of the Moabite god." He glanced at his young sons. "But, no more talk of Chemosh. Did you find us a house?"

Naomi was not placated. "I would never live in one of their houses! The homes and surroundings are beautiful, but only because they are built on the misery of other human beings. One of the slaves I saw might have been my own mother. I beg of you, please, please, don't ask me to live in a Moabite city!"

Her husband drew her into his arms. "Don't be distressed, darling. I understand your feelings. We'll live as we did that first summer of our marriage—in tents, on the open fields. We'll go into the cities only when we need to."

A few days later, encamped in a green pastureland not far from the city, Elimelek said, "By my count, today is the Sabbath."

"So it is," replied Naomi.

"Then I will carry on my observance of our day of rest as I did in Bethlehem. Mahlon and I will go to the gates and visit with the townsmen. What will you and Chilion do?"

"We, too, will rest, while we watch the sheep."

Father and son returned at dusk, bubbling with excitement. "Did we have luck!" Elimelek said. "In the marketplace Mahlon and I struck up a conversation with a Moabite and his sons and found we had much in common. The man invited us to a place of learning, and out of curiosity we went with them."

"And, Mother, they took us to a grove where we sat before a teacher."

"What did you learn from this teacher?" she asked.

"There's a way of counting the days, months, and years that's different from ours. They call their method a calendar: they mark time by the sun, not by the moon as we do it. This is the way they figure . . ." and the boy repeated what he had heard.

Elimelek was pleased at how well Mahlon had learned the lesson. "Chilion, would you like to come with us next Sabbath?"

Chilion's shining eyes were answer enough.

The following Sabbath when father and sons returned from their day in the king's city, it was Chilion who ran up to Naomi to tell her about his day with the Moabites. "Mother! I learned to wrestle!"

"Wrestle? But you did that all the time at home with your friends."

Elimelek explained, "After the lesson in the grove, our Moabite friends took us to their public baths, a large building where men and boys exercise. The people of Moab take their sports seriously. Even wrestling is an art, very different from child's play."

The third Sabbath Elimelek surprised his wife by saying, "Today after the class and the games at the baths, our friends entertained us in their home."

Naomi hesitated. "Do you think you and the boys should go into their homes? After inviting you to partake of their education and sports and hospitality, will they next invite you to join them in their worship of Chemosh?"

"Naomi! Don't you know me better? I tell you my new friends are fine gentlemen. I'm flattered that they enjoy our company. As for worshipping Chemosh, have no fear. When they talk of their gods, it is with a touch of scorn. So, one subject we don't discuss is their religion, or mine."

His answer satisfied Naomi. From then on, life in Moab was harmonious in its rhythm of six days of laboring with their growing herd of sheep, and on the seventh day resting in the company of educated Moabites. In their quest for green pasturelands from one end of Moab to the other, they became well acquainted with the inhabitants of the cities and villages, and in each place made good friends.

Naomi was so unaware of the passing of time that she was both surprised and amused one day to hear Mahlon's voice suddenly hit a high note, then just as abruptly drop low. They all laughed about it, especially when, a few months later, Chilion's did the same.

"They are becoming men," she said. "Soon they will have beards and think of getting married. Oh, if only there were Judean girls about . . ."

By the time both boys were eighteen they were fully-bearded, handsome men who were known throughout Moab as honest, intelligent, peace-loving shepherds.

Mahlon was ever more like his father, kindly and serious. His calm eyes and thoughtful speech made him appear shy; he loved solitude, talked little, and listened much. He was happy to be a shepherd, to live in unhindered freedom with nature.

Chilion was his brother's opposite. Taller than his father and his brother, he possessed great personal magnetism and loved company. Curly-haired and merry-eyed, he was as quick to respond to flirtatious girls as he was, in anger, to aggressive and unfriendly shepherds.

"Chilion," Elimelek sometimes chided, "whenever I am not along to help you and your brother move the herd, I hear news that you have broken the peace."

His younger son grinned. "Can I help it, Father, if people talk about me? I like people, especially women, and most men too, unless they try to best me."

"Why don't you try talking in a calm way when other shepherds get ahead of you to the wells and the herbage, before you swing your fists?"

"Father, you know we always try the reasonable way. Mahlon does the talking to those ox-heads, but I get angry when I see them take advantage and get ahead of us because he is trying to be peaceful."

"He's honest, Father," said Mahlon. "He lets me do the talking, but we both end up having to protect our rights with our fists."

Teasingly, Chilion added, "As for the women, I won't say I like all the women, just the short, pretty ones who dance."

"And why those?" Naomi couldn't help asking.

"It's the wiggling way they move," answered her irrepressible son. "Why don't you ask Mahlon about the kind he prefers? His problem is that he has only one girl."

Mahlon shrugged. "Chilion has a loose tongue. I like quiet women, and even though I know as many women as he does, I have met only one who shares my thinking."

Naomi knew better than to ask more questions, but her curiosity was aroused, and her worry. That night, lying on the mat beside her husband, she whispered so as not to awaken her sons, who were asleep on the other side of the curtain that separated the goat's-hair tent into two bedrooms. "Elimelek, are you awake?"

"Yes."

"What was that talk about Mahlon's and Chilion's girls?"

"Just talk."

"Elimelek, please!"

"Naomi, I know what you're thinking . . . our sons are ready for marriage. I have dallied because in the back of my mind was the hope that somehow we could get Judean wives for them. But even though God has allowed us to prosper, I have never found anyone to trust on such a mission. And now, it's too late. Our sons have made their own choices."

"How do you know? Who are the girls?"

"One is Orpah, and one is Ruth, girls who have known our boys since their fathers invited us into their homes years ago. I have always liked both girls, even though they are as different in personality as our sons are different."

"Oh."

"Don't say 'oh' in that disheartened way. The fathers are good friends of mine whom I respect and admire. Long ago they told me of their willingness to have their daughters marry Judean boys. It so happens that today's conversation, among other things, has forced me to a decision. If I'm right, that Mahlon and Chilion wish to take these Moabite girls for wives, I will make the arrangements immediately."

"What do you mean, 'among other things'?"

But already Elimelek was clutching his chest. Naomi had to struggle to help him up. Shuddering, he forced out the words "Naomi . . . my love . . . tell the boys . . ." and with a horrible choking he slipped out of her arms.

Naomi's sobs shattered the night's silence.

Naomi sat under the shade of the tent awning. She was weaving goat's hair into cloth on a ground loom and keeping watch over the herd. Her tears fell unheeded while she moved the shuttle back and forth.

Nine days before, she and her sons had buried Elimelek in a cave and blocked the opening with huge stones to protect the corpse from prowling animals. For seven days afterward they had mourned their loss. On the eighth day the boys rose and carried out Elimelek's plan for their marriages. On this day they were bringing home the brides.

Naomi cried, but not for Elimelek alone. *My beloved, why did you leave me at this time? You would have told me . . . should I give our tent to our eldest son and his wife since they are now the rightful heads of this family? Will Mahlon's wife want me here? Moabite women may have no use for widows or mothers-in-law in their homes.*

It was dusk when at last she saw Mahlon and Chilion pulling the lead donkeys the brides rode on. Behind them plodded two long strings of sheep, goats, and well-laden asses. Naomi's spirits rose. Her sons had married well. She wiped away her tears and put on a smile.

The first to dismount was Mahlon's wife. *How fair she is,* Naomi thought. *How lovely her features. And her clothes are beautiful.*

The girl was slender and almost as tall as Naomi. She looked golden, from her light brown hair and eyes to the pale yellow veil banded by a costly crown hung with Mahlon's gold coins. The dress, necklaces, and wide chain encircling her waist were simple yet exquisitely fashioned.

Without awkwardness or hesitation the girl reached for Naomi's hand and kissed it. In a voice as tranquil as her eyes, she said, "I am Ruth, your daughter."

The Judean woman, at first taken aback by the hand kissing, now embraced the girl warmly. Ruth's action and words had let Naomi know what her place in the household would be: she would be the matriarchal head of the house of Hezron in Moab. "Welcome into the family of Elimelek," Naomi said, and she kissed Ruth's forehead.

As Ruth stepped back, Chilion's wife, Orpah, presented herself. Her dress was elaborate with long ribbons, colored braid, and heavy embroidery; little bells tinkled from her crown, her earrings, and her golden anklets. Orpah reminded Naomi of someone . . . who? Who had the same vivacious black eyes and short, voluptuous figure that swayed sensuously as she walked?

Tirza! Aunt Tirza in her young wifehood! Naomi opened her arms wide as she did when embracing her aunt and kissed Orpah with unquestioning love.

Happiness intoxicated them all. Mahlon said, "Mother, you and the girls prepare the wedding feast. Chilion and I will get a lamb ready for roasting, just as Father would."

That night, seated before the smiling, kissing couples, partaking of the feast, Naomi's heart spoke to her God: *Eternal One, You have taken away my beloved husband, but You have given me two others to fill the void. From these four, may many children issue, and may Elimelek's name live on.*

The wedding meal lasted late into the night as the newlyweds had much to tell Naomi, but at last the men asked their wives, "Where shall we erect our tents?"

Ruth and Orpah answered together, "On either side of Mother's."

In the morning Naomi helped the girls unpack. They opened Ruth's possessions first and spread out thick-piled rugs, securing upright the hand-wrought braziers that would give heat and light in the tent. Naomi and Orpah praised Ruth's household articles and clothing for their fine quality.

Then they went to Orpah's tent. Excitedly, Orpah opened all her chests and bags at once. Naomi turned white.

"Orpah, what are these?"

"Oh, they are Chemosh and Ashtoresh," she answered innocently. "They are my father's household gods and I love them so much he gave them to Chilion and me for wedding presents."

Naomi felt sick. "Orpah, Ruth, there's been so much excitement since last night and I'm a little tired now. Please go on with your unpacking."

To quiet their concern she added, "I'll be fine after I've rested a while."

Naomi lay on her mat, thinking. *I should tell Orpah that I condemn her gods, gods who would kill her own children. Yet, if I say this to her, she may become angry.* Her thoughts wandered. *Before Elimelek came into my life, I hated everyone. Now I love and want to be loved, especially by my new daughters. So how can I win their love and understanding if I criticize their gods? Perhaps . . . perhaps when Chilion sees the idols in his tent, he will forbid them.*

But after a few weeks' time Naomi realized that Chilion was so in love he was oblivious of all but his wife.

Naomi was torn with indecision. *Should I choose to remain silent or speak to Orpah and risk her displeasure?*

It was Orpah who spoke first. She and Naomi were alone at the stream, on their knees, washing clothes. "Mother, you have been so quiet of late, not joining in our conversations at night, not teaching Ruth and me any more of your Judean ways."

Naomi took a deep breath. "Orpah, I . . . I was pondering something about the ways of our God, who lives in such contrast to Chemosh and Ashtoresh. I have seen that the gods of Moab live in luxuriously appointed marble halls. Their worshippers hear soft music there, smell perfumed incense, and admire the beauty of the human form in nude statues."

"Where does your god live?" Orpah asked.

"He is unseen; there are no carved statues of Him. His only symbol is a small wooden ark containing stone tablets with His laws inscribed on them."

Orpah looked puzzled. "Only a small ark with laws?"

"His laws appeal to the mind and the heart. For example: Israelites must honor not only parents but neighbors and strangers, too."

The young woman stopped beating the clothes and listened intently.

"Our God commands that there be no killing, stealing, or envying another man's possessions, including his wife. Bearing false witness, cheating, committing adultery are sins against other human beings. Every seventh day, man and his beasts of burden must rest. Above all He commands that we should have no other gods around Him. He is the only God."

Naomi paused. Could she risk making her daughter-in-law angry? "Dear Orpah," she said, "I ask you . . . I ask you to remove the Moabite gods."

For a long while Orpah sat in deep thought. Naomi waited for the stinging words that would drive her away from her sons.

At last the girl spoke. "Mother, my idols have been good to me. They brought me Chilion whom I love dearly. True, Chilion objected to my gods, but I persuaded him that when I bear him a son, he will see how generous they are.

"But I love Chilion more than my gods. I will not bring any more unhappiness to him, or to you, because of them."

Naomi's tears mingled with Orpah's as they hugged in love and understanding.

That night before the campfire, Naomi spoke of the teachings of her God and how His laws affected the Judean people in their progress from slavery to tribal freedom. She told them of her father-in-law's dream of the tribes' uniting into a nation to preserve their freedom.

With the passing years, Naomi's admiration for her daughters grew. Orpah's gaiety and constant chatter were balanced by Ruth's few words and restful silences. Yet each girl had the outstanding qualities that made her husband happy, and Naomi considered herself blessed, in every way but one.

Oh, Eternal One, she prayed, *it has been three years since my sons married, and no child has been granted them. Have I brought the curse of my barrenness to my sons' wives? Are there to be no inheritors, no one to carry on Elimelek's name?*

The answer became obvious when, in the ensuing decade, the couples remained childless. Not wishing to oppress Mahlon and Chilion with their tears, the women learned to wait until the men were away, then they wept and prayed and found comfort in each other.

It was again the season of the year when the Judean shepherds prepared to leave the mountains for the grassy meadows of Moab's plateaus. On the sun-drenched slopes, the herds nibbled up the last blades of herbage. Naomi, Ruth, and Orpah filled pouches, bags, and baskets for the journey while the men were a short distance away with the herd, examining them before setting out for the long march.

Suddenly, as she worked, Naomi had a premonition of danger. The breeze died down, the air became leaden, the sun clouded over, and its rays lost their heat within minutes. The bright greens and yellows of the mountainsides turned an ominous gray. The sky darkened quickly and a cold wind began to stir. Naomi felt its icy breath against her bare arms and legs.

She trembled. She knew that nature sometimes became unpredictable and brought rare snow storms.

"Ruth, Orpah! Hurry! Put on your sheepskin coats! Get coats to the men! A blizzard is coming!"

The young women dropped their work, put on the furry coats, and ran to the slopes with coats for their thinly clad husbands. Naomi scrambled into her coat as she dashed to drive the farthest sheep into caves before they froze to death in the open.

As she ran, Naomi felt the temperature plunge; with it, the wind rose and strengthened until it became a swirling force that brought snow in large, sodden flakes. Before she was halfway up the slope, the slashing snow drew clouds of sand into its current and thickened the mixture into a dense fog that dropped like a curtain around the lone woman. Hundreds of bone-dry tumbleweeds, broken loose from their moorings, whipped Naomi about the head and body like beating fists.

Hand over face, she twisted and turned away from the punishing weeds, screaming, "Help! Help! Here I am! Help me!"

The wind forced the breath back into her mouth and she swallowed grit, sand, and snow. She moved her legs but had no sensation of walking. Her naked feet felt frozen.

I must find the children . . . I must keep moving . . . to find them.

She stumbled and fell to her knees. Tears of helplessness blinded her eyes. At that moment, an ice-hardened tumbleweed struck her chest with such force it knocked her over. She lay on the packed snow, unable to open her eyes, her hands and feet frozen. She knew that death was near.

It was hours before the freak blizzard finally subsided. The wind calmed down and the sun came out, bright and hot, melting the snow rapidly. Ruth and Orpah had been searching for Naomi and finally found her. They carried her to a dry spot, where they rubbed her body until warmth returned.

Naomi opened her eyes to see the young women's tear-swollen, wind-burned faces hovering anxiously over hers. Naomi read the terrible news in their eyes.

"My sons!"

"When we found them, it was too late," they sobbed. "Their bodies lay beside the dead sheep."

Naomi lay dazed, trying to comprehend the enormity of the truth. "Show me where they are," she cried. "We must hide them. The ravaging beasts must not find them!"

The young women led her to Mahlon and Chilion and the three of them carried the corpses to a nearby cave. There was no time to weep. Already the herd's death yard was becoming the feasting ground for wolves and jackals. The women had time only to close and kiss the eyes of the dead men. Driven by fear for their loved ones, they found unimagined strength and dislodged a huge slab of stone. They succeeded in moving it from the face of the mountain, then pushed it over and over on itself until, with one last mighty heave, they upended it. With a clang, they sealed the opening of the cave forever. Mahlon and Chilion could sleep in eternal safety.

But there was not yet safety for the women. The ghoulish visitors of the field were becoming so numerous that there was snarling and fighting among them over the carcasses of the herd. If there was not enough dead to satisfy the preying beasts, they would start attacking the living.

Naomi viewed the distance between the graveyard and the remains of their camp. "We may have just enough time to pick up whatever we can find and get to the highway before the beasts get to us."

They ran to the remnants of the camp, found a slingshot, a knife, and some shoes. Swiftly they fled from the scene of so much tragedy. Not until they ceased to hear the sounds of the grisly banquet did they stop to catch their breaths. Then they gave vent to their grief, crying as the walked.

Naomi stumbled. The girls were immediately at her side. "Mother, are you all right?" they asked.

"Oh, my poor daughters! Forgive me, I have been crying for my loss . . . but you . . . what should we do? Where are we going?"

Ruth and Orpah had no answer; they shook their heads.

And as usual, Naomi faced the problem. She had to decide at once how to care for them all. But how could she care for anyone? What could she provide?

I have nothing. I can do nothing for them, or for myself, for we are alike: three unwanted widows. I can't even offer them a home in Bethlehem, because I have none there.

For Naomi, the only home she was entitled to was the sepulcher of her father when she died. Elimelek's property, after so many years, would have been claimed lawfully by other Hezronites, blood-kinsmen to her father-in-law, Natan. The three widows, not having been blood relatives, would indeed be given a sorry welcome by the present occupants should they show themselves there.

I owe my life to my daughters, Naomi thought. *They have given me unstinting loyalty. Better that I release them from any feelings of obligation to me. They can return, without remorse, to their homes where, with the advantageous background of wealthy fathers and brothers, they will soon have husbands again.*

"Mother! See, on the horizon. A caravan is coming! Oh, we are in luck!" cried Orpah.

"Put your heavy coats down, my daughters," said Naomi. "There's a pressing matter I want to speak about."

They did so, and Naomi laid gentle hands on their shoulders. Sadness and love for them softened her voice: "I have only this short time with you, so please, hear me out."

Wonderingly, the girls waited.

"I wish you to go, Ruth and Orpah, and return to the homes of your birth. I pray that God will deal kindly with you, as you have dealt with your husbands and me. May He grant that you find loving husbands, so that once again each of you may be mistress in your own home."

Ruth's reddened eyes were wide with surprise. "On, no!"

"We want to go back with you to your people," said Orpah.

"Don't make a mockery of me," Naomi pleaded. "Go your own way. If I should say that I had hopes of marrying, even if I had a husband this night and bore sons, would you wait for them until they are grown? Would you let that keep you from marrying now while you are still beautiful and can arouse men to desire you for wives?

"No, my daughters, I am burdened with even greater sorrow for your sakes, knowing that God has made a useless spectacle of me. For my sake, turn back, return to your fathers' homes."

Orpah cried aloud, but seeing that Naomi's determination was unshakable, she threw her arms around her Judean mother and kissed her farewell.

The caravan, moving slowly and steadily, had just passed the three women. Naomi drew Orpah once more closely to her, reluctant to let her go. It was as if Tirza, in the person of Orpah, was leaving her to face life alone again.

Orpah picked up her coat and ran after the caravan-masters. When she asked for permission to follow in their group, the kindly traders granted her their protection.

"Ruth! Come along!" she called back.

Naomi drew Ruth into her arms, sympathizing with this kindly girl to whom words did not come easily. Ruth rested her head on Naomi's shoulder, as she had always done. In a little while, seeing the caravan begin to recede in the distance, Naomi put her hand under Ruth's chin. "Look up, turn your head, Ruth. See, your sister-in-law is going back to her people and her gods. Go with her."

The young woman looked up into Naomi's face.

"No. Don't tell me to leave you and turn back from following you. Where you go, I will go. Where you stay, I will stay. Your people will be my people, and your God, my God. Wherever you die, there will I die, and beside you, I will be buried. May God kill me and worse, if anything but death were to part you and me!"

No! No! was Naomi's dismayed reaction. *She can't mean it! She doesn't know what she's saying!* Naomi turned away from the girl to hide her confusion. She had to think. It never occurred to her that Ruth would not do as Orpah had done. Why, oh why, would Ruth choose an uncertain life with her mother-in-law when she was free to return to the haven of her parents' home? What kind of misguided loyalty was this?

Yet, could she turn down Ruth's offer, turn away the only human being who wanted her, loved her? Naomi had to make a choice: should she be selfish? Should she keep Ruth with her, to work at hard labor for years perhaps, until both could save enough money to return to Bethlehem without being paupers? And once there, would Ruth experience humiliating treatment as a Moabitess in Bethlehem? How would Ruth survive the cruelties of being a Moabite widow among the Hebrews in Judah?

No! No! Naomi decided. But when she turned to confront her daughter-in-law, the refusal on her lips, she encountered the young woman's self-possessed, steadfast gaze. Never had she seen Ruth look so unyielding. The wet, gold-brown eyes were dark with determination, the defiant mouth and chin declared that she was prepared to refute any argument Naomi would give. Here was a side of Ruth her mother-in-law had never seen. Docile, well-bred, serene Ruth could fight?

Without a word, Naomi stooped and picked up her coat. Ruth did the same. Silently, the two women started the long, long journey home. And Naomi thought, *What now is in store for us?*

Book 2

NAOMI

AND

RUTH

.

They walked on a rutted, stony road in a lonely wasteland. The angular Avarim Mountains were getting smaller, the site of Mahlon's and Chilion's tomb lost to view in the misty clouds hanging overhead.

As Naomi and Ruth searched the bleak, darkening landscape for shelter for the night, they saw two herdsmen leading a mass of sheep. The men were peasants, as dirty gray as their herd, dressed in crudely sewn sheepskins. They stared at the two unprotected females—surprise, then lust glinting in their eyes.

There was no time to run, no place for escape.

Naomi whispered to Ruth, "Get behind me. Throw one sleeve as a cover over your face. With the other hand, hold onto my girdle. Utter no word, no matter what I say!"

And stretching forth her palms as if to prevent contact, Naomi cried loudly, "Leper! Leper! Abomination! Leper!"

There was no mistaking the awful warning. The men cursed but made a wide circle away from the two women.

When the men and sheep had melted into the twilight, the women fell into each other's arms. "Oh, Mother, you knew what to do! You knew!"

"Believe me, my child, I'm as surprised as you are that my wits suddenly came alive!"

They spent the night where they were, huddled together, and rose with the dawn. As they resumed walking, Ruth said, "I will ask at the first farmhouse if I can help with the work. Perhaps they will pay with food."

They walked many hours, but the area was wild country, uninhabited and unfit for agriculture. Naomi walked slower and slower, fatigue and hunger sapping her vitality.

"I'm weary, Ruth. Let's rest."

"Mother, look! There, beyond the rise of land, I see men working. I'll ask them for work."

"Wait! I'll go with you. You mustn't go alone."

They walked toward the place where perhaps a hundred men were clearing and leveling a section of land. Teams of oxen dragged away boulders while slaves hammered apart huge clumps of earth. More slaves were occupied building long barracks. In the midst of the workers, wearing only a loincloth, stood a man shouting orders. When they were close, Naomi saw that he was young, about Mahlon's age, and a most uncommon overseer. There was an air of refinement as well as authority about him, and the eyes in the clean-shaven face were keenly intelligent.

Naomi addressed him, "Good master, we are two widows seeking employment. Please give us work."

Hands on hips, the man regarded her and Ruth in disbelief. "What are you women doing out here alone, so far from the city?"

"We are shepherds' wives. My sons and our herd were killed yesterday in the mountain storm. My name is Naomi. This is my daughter Ruth."

He shook his head. "You are taking great risks in working here. Although I keep the slaves chained at night, the free men may wish to harm you. It would be far safer if you kept going until you reach the city."

Naomi answered simply, "We are hungry. We need work now."

The man shrugged. "I can use extra hands; this land is being prepared for a training camp for the king's soldiers. It will be your task to follow the hammer-men. You will chop the earth as small as possible so our rollers can flatten and smooth the surface. Here, take these mallets and start at this point."

The presence of the women disrupted the workers' concentration until angry orders and crackling whips restored the pace.

Naomi whispered to Ruth, "With all those men staring at us, I feel we're in a lion's den. Don't bind up your skirt."

Ruth nodded. Although the long skirts hampered them, they kept them down.

After three long, hard rows Ruth saw that Naomi's strength was waning. The clay-dry clumps of earth that Naomi chopped were too large for the rollers. Ruth fell behind her, and unknown to Naomi, went over her portion while maintaining her own steady chopping. The king's young overseer saw this, but said nothing.

The sun was high and burning when a shrill whistle blew and work ceased. Breathing heavily, Naomi sat down, head on arms. A slave brought two flat loaves of bread and a jug of vinegar-wine. The coarse bread and sour drink were refreshing and revivifying. Naomi dipped the bread in the vinegar and savored each morsel.

"Ruth, I can feel strength in my limbs. How good it is to earn my food!"

The whistle blew, work was resumed, and Naomi swung her hammer with energy. This time Ruth didn't have to go over her mother-in-law's portion of earth.

The sun was setting when the whistle blew again. The same slave brought parched corn, bread, and vinegar. The women ate in silence, contented.

"You may sleep behind my tent. No one will come near to molest you."

Naomi and Ruth looked up. The overseer stood over them, whip in hand. His face and voice were impersonal, and before they could thank him, he was gone.

One night, at the end of the first week, Naomi said, "My daughter, this exhausting work is my salvation. To give an honest day's work takes all my strength. Each night I fall into such deep sleep, I have no time to think or mourn."

The next night she said, "Ruth, have you noticed that our portion of bread and vinegar is more generous each day?"

Ruth didn't answer. She was fast asleep.

The night after, they found two rush mats behind the overseer's tent. "What luxury!" exulted Naomi. "To have a mat to stretch out on!"

Naomi wanted to thank the young man, but there was no opportunity. She knew Ruth was the reason he extended these kindnesses. Often at work, when she straightened up to ease her back, she caught the overseer's eyes on her daughter-in-law; there was a sad, lonely expression on his face.

One night as they relaxed on their mats, Naomi whispered, "The overseer is unusual; he's so humane to us."

"It's because we're good workers."

"It's more . . . he's attracted to you."

Ruth didn't answer.

"Ruth, he's a fine man. One of your own kind, a Moabite of high character. If you show him encouragement, perhaps . . . perhaps he would take you for wife."

Her daughter-in-law answered in a troubled voice. "Please, Mother, I'm not interested in marrying, and certainly not a Moabite, since I'm a Judean now. I believe in your God's teachings. I will live only with you in your ways."

Naomi sighed.

After a few weeks, the vast camp was a smooth, hard-surfaced training area. Already hordes of paid mercenaries were arriving along with the king's own troops. The workers' tasks were finished.

Waiting to be paid, Naomi and Ruth were last in line. The overseer said, "You've been honest workers and genteel women in your conduct. I can direct you to other overseers who employ for the king. Where are you going?"

"Bethlehem."

"Bethlehem? You're far from there."

"We'll get there in due time. Right now we would welcome more work," said Naomi.

"The king's winemaker is on the northern road. In two days' walk you'll come to the royal vineyards. The overseer has many slaves, but at this time of the year he can use extra helpers."

Gratefully, the women thanked him, but he seemed reluctant to have them leave. "Are you well-shod? You have a long journey ahead. I see your shoes need clouting." He called to the cobbler-slave, "Here, clout these shoes." He smiled at the women's delighted expressions.

Naomi and Ruth slipped off the worn shoes and watched the cobbler stud the soles with nails. Now, walking on the stony roads would be less painful.

"Master," said Naomi while they waited, "we are thankful for your protection and favors. Our blessings on your good parents for rearing a son like you."

The smile on the young man's face faded. All friendliness gone, he said, "My father is the monarch of all Moab . . . there are many women in his house."

Naomi and Ruth were stunned. He was of royal blood! An illegitimate son of the king! Now it was all clear to Naomi: even though he may have desired Ruth, he was too noble-minded to force her to submit to him, and too nobly born to marry her.

Naomi's heart was saddened for the prince of Moab and the humiliating position of his life.

The women put on their newly clouted shoes, picked up their coats and meager belongings, and set out for the king's vineyards. When they passed the nearby woods, Naomi said, "Ruth, see the wild berries over there! Let's eat all we can, and if we gather more for later, we can save what we've earned for the winter months."

In two days' time, the women saw the king's banners fluttering above broad vineyards. They found their way to the low building where people wanting work waited to be interviewed. When their turn came, the king's overseer asked, "Your name and birthplace?"

"We are Naomi and Ruth from Moab. We have been working in the king's military camp in the south."

"Come closer."

The man raised expressionless eyes and scrutinized the women carefully: no brand marks on the arms, no scars on their necks and ankles from iron chains. They were neither escaping slaves nor runaway bondswomen.

He nodded, checked numbers on long tables, and pointed to Ruth. "You tread grapes in press four."

To Naomi he said, "You stay with the harvesters. If you work well, you can stay the full harvest. One word of warning—don't speak to or help the king's slaves."

He handed Naomi a basket and a small, sharp grape sickle, then waved them both in the direction of their jobs. Mother and daughter looked at each other in quiet joy: if they could work the full grape-gathering and wine-making season, they could earn enough to go home without delay.

Naomi joined the older workers and slaves who cut the ripe fruit. When their baskets were full, they dumped them into one of the many presses dotting the vineyard.

The presses were large, cleared areas with adjoining storage pits dug low in the earth and lined smoothly with mortar. Through channels, the juice of the foot-crushed grapes in the presses flowed down into the storage pits.

When Naomi's first basket was full, she went to the press where Ruth worked, her skirt bound high into her belt. The seven men and women working there in short tunics and bare feet were already drunk with fermented wine. They trampled the grapes, arms around each other, and sang bawdily. Ruth did not see Naomi, for she was turned away, working alone.

At day's end, when work ceased and food was brought, Ruth said, "Mother, let's not eat with the others. Why don't we go into the women's quarters and eat?"

"But it's so depressing in there."

The building housing the itinerant women workers was a partitioned half of a long, narrow prison where, on the other side, the chained slaves were locked every night.

"It's quiet there, away from the noise and sight of those dreadful people in the press. We can enjoy being alone, before they come in to sleep."

"What about those people? Are they abusing you?"

"No . . . it's their talk and obscene songs that disturb me."

"I'll keep watch over you, my child, but call out loudly if you're in trouble."

The day after, bent over a thickly grown vine, Naomi heard a woman's screams. Instantly, she stood erect, eyes searching the press. Ruth was not there! Naomi's fingers tightened on the grape sickle as she ran toward the sound of the screams.

Then she saw her. Ruth was struggling to free herself from the arms of a burly grape treader. He was carrying her toward the far side of the orchard where the vines were thickest. In spite of her shrieks, no one stopped the man or attempted to save the girl. Workers and slaves didn't look up from their tasks, nor did the overseer intervene.

Naomi's first impulse was to run after the abductor and plunge the sickle into his back. But she knew he would overpower her.

My slingshot . . . I'll use my slingshot!

Naomi blessed Elimelek for training her to be a shepherd's wife. She withdrew the sling from her girdle, fitted a small jagged stone in it, and waited. When she could see the man's head in the open, she began to whirl the sling slowly, then with ever increasing speed until she discharged the missile with accurate aim. It struck the back of the peasant's head and he dropped instantly, toppling over on Ruth.

Quickly, Naomi ran to the girl and helped her roll the man off. "Run for the highway!" she said. "Keep away from the buildings! Don't stop for anyone or anything!"

They ran between rows of vines to the highway and kept running. In the distance were farm buildings and stable doors wide open. They climbed up into a hayloft, collapsed on the straw, and lay there, breathing heavily, hearts pounding.

"Ruth, are you all right?"

"Yes, Mother, oh, yes! I'm happy to be gone from that place."

"I'm glad, too. I know I only stunned that beast, but the king's police will be searching for us. We'll hide for a few days."

After a while Ruth whispered in a wondering tone, "Mother, how did your stone find its mark so unerringly?"

"I controlled my anger so that my hand wouldn't lose its sureness."

"I'm so proud of you."

Naomi smiled ruefully. "I have a confession: I enjoyed the feeling of power it gave me to see that horrible man fall."

"You saved me," said Ruth, giving Naomi a hug.

"Sh-h-h-h!"

Oxen bells clanged in the road. The women slipped out of the barn and hid in a pile of hay just as the farmer led his cattle in. Then they ran through orchards and fields by moonlight. When dawn came, they hid behind another stable. When the owner and his field workers led the cattle out, the two ran in.

"Mother, I'm hungry and thirsty. Do you think we're likely to be followed this far from the king's vineyard? Could we go out and search for food?"

"We're in luck, Ruth. Look there!"

Naomi, peering over the mangers, pointed to a squat barrel of rainwater and a sack of parched corn.

"The men must have forgotten their food and water," Ruth said.

"No. It just means that someone will be here for them before the sun is high. Let's drink and eat only what we need: you go first, and I'll stand watch."

Ruth crept to the barrel, drank, then took a small handful of the whole roasted corn.

When it was Naomi's turn, she cupped the water in her hands as she knelt over the barrel . . . and saw her reflection.

She spilled back the water. *No! That can't be me!*

She looked at herself again and pushed the loosened hair away from her face. It was a grim-faced, hollow-eyed Naomi who looked back at her. Her once full, expressive lips were thin and unsmiling. Her eyes were dull, and her skin as rippled with wrinkles as the water when she disturbed it.

She straightened up, hating the reflection. She smoothed her disheveled hair and held the long braids in her hands: they too were lifeless, gray, old.

How ugly she had become! And now she so urgently needed the ornamentation of physical beauty when they returned to Judah. Not only was her status that of a widow, but she was an unlovely one. She had no allure left. She would never marry again.

Suddenly she was very tired. Her shoulders sagged with loathing at the repulsive changes that age and a punishing nature had brought her. She was weary of life.

I wish I could go back to Bethlehem, she thought, *so I could die there and be buried with my father.*

"Mother!" came Ruth's loud whisper. "Are you all right? Bring your food. I'm waiting."

Naomi returned with her corn. Munching on hers, Ruth said, "You had the strangest look on your face as you knelt by the water barrel."

"My thoughts were strange. I never want to see my reflection again."

"Why?"

"When I saw what I look like now, I lost my confidence, my will to live. I saw only ugliness."

"You're not ugly!" Ruth said. "The light that shines in your eyes is radiant, and the kindness and wisdom I see in them is attractive. Nature may have changed your hair and features but it could never wither your courage or crush your spirit. I think you're beautiful."

"Ah, Ruth . . . Ruth. Only you could restore my crumpled vanity and inspire me to keep going. Bless you."

After a short rest Naomi suggested, "We're far enough from the king's vineyard. Let's go and find work."

Since it was the season of the year when the grapes and olives were at their ripest, they were hired without question to help with the harvesting.

"If only we had our sheepskin coats," said Naomi more than once. "I'm chilled to the bone every night."

The work was hard. Many times Naomi fainted, overcome with fatigue from the cold, uncomfortable nights and the long work days. Then Ruth would revive her with vinegar-wine soaked in a rag and held to her lips.

And just as often, Ruth would scream out, "Mother! Mother!" Then the master or the worker abducting the young woman would feel a knife in his back or a sharp stone cracking his skull. These men never saw that it was a gray-haired woman who was their attacker because she and Ruth were fast to escape.

"Ah, daughter," Naomi would say, "it will take us a long time to save enough money to go home."

"Don't worry, Mother, as long as we're together."

One night, unable to sleep from overexhaustion, the two women talked.

"Ruth, I've watched you a long time now and your actions puzzle me. Men are quickly drawn to you, yet I never see you speak to them."

Ruth replied simply, "My love was buried with Mahlon. I can ignore all other men."

"How little I've understood you. You've been like a stream, flowing tranquilly on the surface, yet with unknown depths."

"It's why I want always to be with you, Mother. You are all of Mahlon I have left. I see him in your expressions, your speech, your thoughts. Nothing must ever happen to you because then all I loved in the world would be gone."

"I will never leave you," Naomi said. "We will live and die together."

They worked and hoarded their money until the day arrived when they began the long walk to Bethlehem. When they descended the mountainside road to the river gorge where, some twenty years before, Mahlon had wanted to stay, Naomi said, "I feel as though I were here yesterday. Nothing is changed. The gorge is as lovely as before: even the butterflies look the same."

They came out of the gorge to the low-lying plain on the eastern side of the Dead Sea. By traveling through the villages northward, they would reach the narrow spot where the Jordan River emptied into the sea. There they would cross to Judah on a ferry, walk to Jericho, and turning southward again, head for Jerusalem and Bethlehem.

"Ruth, see the olive orchards surrounding the villages? Harvesters are swarming in them. The fruit must be ripe. We'll find plenty of work for the asking before we go home."

Naomi was hired, along with aged slaves and young children, to collect the fallen olives in deep baskets. Ruth joined a group of strong, young people who beat the ripe olives from the trees with long-poled tools.

Naomi and her group carried the filled baskets to a large, stone basin. There, the olives were crushed by a huge, circular vertical millstone revolving on a long beam attached to a pivot. An ox was harnessed to the long beam: it plodded in a dirt ring, rounding the millstone that pressed out the oil, which drained smoothly into tall, storage jars. The remaining pulp, still holding a quantity of oil, was taken to smaller presses where every drop was squeezed out.

Then the young people beat the trees a second time.

Naomi voiced her disapproval. "In Bethlehem, as in all Judah, we never allowed the workers to beat the trees a second time."

"Why not?" asked Ruth. "Wasn't that wasteful?"

"It wasn't waste, it was charity. The Law says that the second beating should be left for the needy: the widows, the aged, the orphans. It's their only means of oil supply for cooking, heating, and lighting. The same Law applies to the grain harvests: the corners of the field as well as the droppings of the harvesters must be left for the poor to glean."

The two women took whatever jobs they could find while always moving northward. The winter was almost over when Naomi said, "Tomorrow we cross the Jordan River as proud women returning home," but as she spoke, her heart was torn between eagerness and fear.

CHAPTER 15

As they waited on the bank of the river for the raft to ferry them across, Naomi said, "Here is where we walked over the Jordan. The drought was so prolonged then that the mighty waters of this river were mere trickles."

The Jordan was a thrilling sight to Ruth, who was seeing it for the first time. In all of Moab there was no body of water so extensive as this one.

When they landed on the Judean side of the Jordan and Ruth observed the city and people of Jericho, she exclaimed, "Everyone is so friendly here! Even the palm trees seem to wave their welcome to us."

Naomi reflected, "The first time I saw Jericho, the people were not so friendly. They closed their doors to us. Let's see if we can find my friend Kezia's relatives."

They inquired, but Kezia's relatives were gone. The old kinspeople had died, and the young ones had scattered to other cities.

"Mother, even though we don't know anyone, let's stay here for a day. It's so beautiful."

"Not now, Ruth. I'm consumed with restlessness."

When they came within sight of Jerusalem, rising majestically on its hill, Naomi felt for the first time that she was nearing home. To the two travelers gazing up at the high walls of the famous city, Jerusalem appeared to be the very crest of spring: its slopes, softly green, sprouted new grass.

That night they went to sleep in an orchard. The next morning, when the women shook the sleep from their eyes, the almond trees had opened their buds and stood fully bedecked with rosy-white flowers.

"Look!" said Naomi. "The trees are telling us that it's spring."

The women walked spellbound through the countryside, for the whole landscape was riotous with color: barley fields were yellow with early ripening grain; where the plow had not uprooted them, the blue flowers of the creeping flax plants perked up their heads; anemones sprang up where only grass was apparent the night before; the hillsides were ablaze with mock roses and poppies; and from crevices in the rocks on the mountain slopes bloomed clusters of cyclamen.

Ruth was so overwhelmed with the sight and sound of burgeoning spring that she walked as in a dream. It was a while before she realized her mother-in-law was dragging her feet and falling behind.

She ran back to Naomi. "Mother, what's the matter? Aren't you happy to see all this? Isn't the stream over there familiar to you?"

Tears fell from Naomi's eyes. "Yes, I know the stream. But to me, it could be the Dead Sea, filled with *marah*, bitter water. My heart is filled with bitterness because of all that is lost to me: Elimelek, Mahlon, Chilion . . . everything is bitter!"

Ruth put her arm around her mother-in-law and held her up as they walked. People filled the road. Naomi wiped her eyes and peered into the strange faces, but she knew no one. Suddenly she sat down by the wayside, unwilling to go further.

"I should not have come back," she said. "No one knows me. There's no one to call me by name. I'm a stranger among my own." She seemed to shrink into herself; she looked older and grayer than before, her eyes swollen.

"Mother, come. When we are in Bethlehem, it will be better."

By late afternoon they reached the well outside the town. It looked the same, surrounded by chattering townspeople drawing the night's supply of water. Silence fell when the two strangers approached. They stared when the old woman asked no questions but went directly into the well enclosure. With complete familiarity, she dropped the leather bucket, drew water, and knew the exact spot where the stone ledge curved to hold the bucket from tipping. Filling the clay dipper, she offered her companion a drink, at the same time applying wet fingers to her reddened eyes.

The city women, curious but hesitant to greet strangers, said nothing, until a silvery haired one disengaged herself from the group and gazed into the face of the old woman.

"Naomi!"

Naomi dropped her hands. She knew the strident voice. It was Kezia! The sight of her friend's face with the sharp, black eyes broke Naomi's composure. She fell into Kezia's arms. "Call me not Naomi, the name of pleasantness. Call me Marah, for God has dealt bitterly with me. I went out of Bethlehem full of pride; I had a husband and two sons. And now God has brought me back, empty."

Kezia said nothing, but held her friend close.

Naomi cried herself out, then raised her head and saw Ruth standing by, waiting.

Stricken, Naomi reached for Ruth's hand and drew her into an embrace. She said to Kezia, "In my relief at seeing you, I neglected the only blessing left me: this is Mahlon's wife, Ruth. If it were not for her, I would never have reached Bethlehem; I would surely have died on the way. Ruth, of Moabite birth, is more precious to me than a blood-daughter."

Kezia studied Ruth in her keen way, then nodded approvingly. "You have the features of a Moabitess, but the soul of a Judean. I welcome you as Naomi's daughter."

Hearing Kezia's greeting, the women of Bethlehem crowded around Naomi and Ruth. Where were the husbands? How far had they traveled?

Kezia pulled her old friend aside. "Naomi, what are your plans?"

"We have no plans, no place to go. Ruth could have returned to her wealthy father, but she chose to stay with me. At first, I didn't want her. I was worried about her safety, but she would have it no other way. We made our way here unaided. We'll find a way to live here, too."

Her friend sighed. "I wish I could offer you a corner in my house. But we are crowded to the doors because my foolish husband decided his timid wives and I were too old for him and has now taken new young wives, and their brats overrun the house and yard."

Naomi smiled. Kezia was unchanged. "For your goodwill, Kezia, we are grateful. But Ruth and I will manage. We can always go to the caves. I remember them well."

"You can't go to the caves, Naomi. When the famine was over so many years ago, vagrant Canaanite and Philistine soldiers came into Bethlehem. They took over the caves as their quarters and brought with them evil women, idols, and lawlessness. Even the Council of Elders can't cope with them. I'll give you money to get lodgings in the gates."

Naomi drew herself up. "Thank you again, Kezia, but we don't need money. We'll take your suggestion and find shelter in town."

Two women came to stand by Kezia's side.

"Meet my good friends, Shulamit and Leah," said Kezia. "They arrived after you left."

The two friends smiled warmly and Naomi liked them immediately. In their company, and Ruth's, Naomi reentered the marketplace she had left so many years before. Then they all said goodnight, and Naomi and Ruth were alone.

"Strange," said Naomi as she glanced about. "Everything is smaller and shabbier than I remember. The stone benches where the elders held court, the watchmen's huts, the auctioneer's block, the market stalls are all so poorly constructed. Even the wooden gates of the city are not so huge or handsome as I once thought."

They found lodging in a small room adjoining the gateman's house. It had mats, stools, and a table, and in a wall-niche were a few cracked bowls and a saucer-shaped lamp. With its wooden beam they barred the door and slept soundly and safely in Bethlehem that night.

They were awakened by the early morning noises: the squeaking and scraping of the gates as they were opened; the voices and laughter of the Judean populace going out of the city to their work.

"It's all the same," Naomi said as she opened the door, "only the faces have changed."

They bought fresh bread in the Bakers' Street and ate it as they walked along. The shops and bazaar were unchanged; only the shopkeepers were different.

"We'll go first to Father Natan's house," Naomi said. But when they approached her husband's home, she grew apprehensive. "Ruth, I'm making a mistake. I'm not brave enough to look at what is no longer ours," and she started to turn back.

"No, Mother," Ruth said firmly, "you must go on. Unless you face it now, you will always want to return here. And I, too, want to see the house where Mahlon was born."

They stood outside Natan's and Malkah's yard, in front of its waist-high stone fence. Women and girls were engrossed in their labors, using the same tools, mills, and bake-oven that Malkah and her daughters and granddaughters had used. The doors of the four homes were closed, but the door Elimelek had made for the sheep pen was open. Naomi breathed a sigh of relief: everything was as she remembered.

None of the women and girls in the yard paid any attention to the strangers at the gate. Naomi called out, "Peace be with you." The women raised their heads, but no one responded.

Naomi continued, "We have just come from a long journey. Please, will you tell us who dwells here?"

Still no answer. After long seconds, one of the women called toward the main house, "Grandmother, a stranger questions us."

A shrewish wisp of an old woman opened Malkah's door. "What do you want?" she asked.

"Will you tell us who dwells here?" asked Naomi again.

The grandmother answered, "Who are you? Why do you want to know?"

"I am Naomi, daughter-in-law of Natan the Hezronite, who dwelt here before the famine."

The old woman marched to the gate, shook it to make sure it was locked, then looked at the two women suspiciously. "My husband may not approve of my talking to you. Where are Natan's sons and grandsons?"

"You don't need to fear us; we're not here to claim anything. My husband and sons are dead."

Reassured, the grandmother became less antagonistic. "We have lived in these houses many years. When the famine ended we learned that Natan's kin did not return. My husband's father was blood-cousin to Natan, both of the Perezites. We took the matter of inheritance to Bethlehem's Council of Elders. They investigated, and finding the blood relationship true, declared my husband Zerah and his family legal heirs of this property."

"Yes, I know that Father Natan belonged to the Perezites. Where was your origin?"

"We were all from Jerusalem."

"All? There were others?"

"My husband's nephew Boaz came too. Boaz happens to be a very rich man," she said proudly. "He bought debtor's fields for his sons and himself, and he has a large dwelling on the other side of the city."

Naomi thought for a moment. "I don't remember hearing Father Natan or Elimelek speak of your husband or his nephew Boaz."

The woman bristled. "I don't care if you heard of us or not. This is our home and our land. No one can dispute that!"

Naomi ignored the old woman and addressed Ruth. "After our marriage, when we returned from months spent away tending the herds and found the city pillaged, Elimelek and I rebuilt all you see." She pointed to the oldest building. "In Mother Malkah's house, Mahlon and Chilion were born."

Ruth nodded as she drank in every detail of Mahlon's birthplace.

The grandmother shook the gate impatiently.

Naomi turned and said, "We will not keep you from your work. Peace be with you."

As they walked away, Naomi smiled ruefully. "The gate that Zerah's wife held shut against us is the very one Elimelek and I defended with our lives against the city's elders!"

"Mother, would you ask them to take us in if we had nowhere else to go?"

"We won't talk of that now. I'm hoping we will find enough work in the barley harvest to sustain us for a long while. Come, there are other places I want you to see."

She and Ruth walked leisurely through familiar streets with Naomi pointing out special sights. After a while Naomi had an uneasy feeling they were being followed. She whirled about: a few yards behind them stood a cluster of men and boys.

What do they want? she wondered, then realized they were not glaring at her—they were glaring at Ruth. Anger flashed through her.

Deliberately, she turned Ruth back and directed her steps past the little mob, while holding one hand over the knife hidden in her belt. She stared the men full in the face, daring them to say the despised word, "Moabitess."

The sullen group stepped back as the women passed, but Naomi saw the menace in their eyes. She had known this might happen and it troubled her deeply.

She led Ruth out of the city to her father's farm. No house was there, just rows of ripe barley on slender stalks waving in the breeze. "It's strange that I can stand before this field and feel no heartache," she said. "As an orphan I seldom came here. Seeing this place sharpened my grief, my loneliness. Now, I recall only the happy days of my childhood. Time for healing is God's legacy." Naomi's voice suddenly rose in excitement. "Ruth! Wait for me here! I won't be long!"

Ruth watched as Naomi ran from one corner of the field to the other. At each corner she looked for something on the ground. When she returned, she cried, "Ruth! Ruth! My father's field markers are untouched, exactly where he left them!"

"What does that mean?"

"It means that my father's land is mine! My legacy! Even if others use it, my father's family still owns it!"

Ecstatically, she threw her arms around her daughter-in-law. Then a second thought sobered her. "Ruth, I may own the land, but I don't own the grain. We'll still have to work to earn our bread and shelter. But, it's important that we attend a meeting of the Council of Elders. We must lose no time claiming our property."

They hurried up the same path that Naomi had run up as a child when she and her aunt warned the town of the enemy attack. Her mind churned with ideas: *What shall I say to them . . . "Honored Men of Bethlehem, may I keep my father's land? Thank you and good-day?" Is that all I'll say? How many chances does a woman get to come into the presence of the ruling elders? Here I have the opportunity of a lifetime. How can I use it to benefit Ruth? What do I want most for her?*

The ideas kept coming. *I know! I want most of all to have Judean doors opened to her, to have my people see her and know her as I do. Then their distrust will vanish. If only I can tell them she's now a Judean, in spirit and belief and behavior, a woman to be respected and honored. If I can do this, perhaps one man in the assembly, seeing her and hearing about her, will want Ruth in marriage.*

The ambitiousness of her project stirred the blood in Naomi's veins. What a way to accomplish her heart's desire for Ruth! To have the council's elders look favorably on Ruth was equal to having the taint of her Moabite birth removed by law.

Trying to keep calm Naomi said, "I've thought of a plan I want to discuss with Kezia. Let's go to her house."

The front yard of Kezia's house was just as she had described it, overrun with children. There were babies of all sizes and ages: laughing, crying, squabbling, while their mothers worked in the midst of the bedlam.

On hearing who was asking for her, Kezia came down from the rooftop and walked through the yard in her regal way.

"Naomi! Ruth! I'm so glad you've come!"

"Kezia, I would like to talk with you, if you have the time."

"I make my own time. Come up to the roof where it is quiet."

A toddler, waddling up to Ruth, fell with a thud on his rear. He howled with hurt surprise and held up his arms to her.

"Oh-h-h, poor little dear!" Ruth picked him up and pressed him close to her. There was such hunger in her grasp that, seeing it, Naomi was saddened. She understood that need for a child. Now, more than ever, she was determined to go through with her plan.

"Would you like to stay here and play with the little one? I won't be long."

Ruth nodded and sat down on the ground to cuddle the little boy. She wiped his tears and rocked him.

"Well," said Kezia when they were alone, "what's on your mind? Your eyes are shining."

"I have just discovered that my father's farm is still mine. Because it's mine, its Ruth's too. Knowing that she is heiress to a piece of land may be of help in getting her a husband."

Kezia's eyes opened wide, but she made no comment.

"It's my plan to present Ruth to the council today. Instead of apologizing for her birthplace, I'll state her virtues, her worthiness, her faith in God. Very few people have met her, but already Ruth is looked upon as a dangerous foreigner. It makes me all the more firm to fight for her chance to live here free from attack and abuse."

Unexpectedly, Kezia laughed. "Let me understand you correctly. You propose to do what perhaps only a prophetess could do, namely, have Bethlehem's men listen with patience and courtesy to the praises of a widow? And a Moabite widow at that? What a jest to play on the pompous elders of the council!"

"Kezia, don't mock me. I know it has never been done, but I have an opening device to gain their attention. Since I have no man to speak for me, only I can claim my inheritance. Then I'll present Ruth as my legal, logical heir."

"So! You've made up you mind. Well, what do you want of me? If it's advice, I can't give you any because what you intend to do is unheard of.

But to ask the Council of Elders to recognize Ruth, using any excuse, may be one way of getting her married, and you a home."

"I know I'm being overbold, Kezia, but if I were young or beautiful enough to marry again, there would be no need to scheme this way. My home would be Ruth's, too. But Ruth is the desirable one, and if she marries, she'll shelter me. If you think me presumptuous to fight for Ruth's chance to marry, it's because you don't know what the widow's portion in life is. I do."

"All right, let it be as you say. How can I help?"

Naomi felt relief. "What I want are clothes for Ruth: a dress and a mantle of fine cloth and design, such as she was accustomed to wearing in Moab."

"Clothes? Well, that's a request easily filled. I'll dress Ruth in a way that will command everyone's admiring attention, especially those men in need of a wife! But, one word of warning, Naomi. Be prepared for the fact that the audience may not be a kind one . . ."

Late that afternoon, Naomi and Ruth left Kezia's house and returned to the marketplace. The elders of the council were already seated on the benches where they were hearing a case. Sitting on the ground before the council was the general assembly made up of relatives, friends, and interested passersby. Waiting their turn, to one side, were the men and witnesses involved in legal disputes.

Since the land of Judah had no king, the council of learned elders was the highest law in each city; it passed judgment on all judicial matters and some religious ones. The ten elders sitting on Bethlehem's bench concurred in their decisions and the supreme elder was spokesman. All sentences were pronounced and carried out in the immediate presence of the council and the assembly. As was the custom, the audience participated vocally in the proceedings.

It was unusual for women to appear there. Even the rare woman who sought a bill of divorcement from a cruel husband would send her father or brother to represent her, rather than brave the scrutiny and comments of the marketplace assembly. Naomi stayed with Ruth in the background until it was her turn to be heard.

The case before the council was that of a wealthy Judean and his

Hebrew slave. The slave refused the freedom that the master wanted to give him and insisted that the master continue to care for him and his large family in return for services rendered. From the assembly rose a rumbling of taunts and threats against the slave. The elders conferred and handed down the decision: Any Hebrew who preferred bondage to freedom would have an awl driven into his ear, to be an object of contempt among free men. Against the background noise of the sneering assembly, the slave had his head placed on a block and a slender awl was driven into the soft lobe of his ear, never to be removed.

Someone in back of Naomi prodded her. "You're next."

Naomi was trembling so hard, Ruth had to help her to her feet. Standing, she glanced over the sea of bearded faces and had an impulse to seize Ruth's hand and run away. But there was no turning back. She came before the elders on the bench and smiled tremulously; there was no responding warmth from them.

In back of her she heard loud mumbling.

"Who are those women?"

"What are they doing here alone?"

"Where is the man who speaks for them?"

Naomi could feel hundreds of eyes boring into her back.

"Speak up, woman! What do you want of the council?"

"I am Naomi," she began, "daughter of Jashuv the Hamulite, who was slain during an attack on Bethlehem. I was his only child. I married Elimelek, son of Natan the Hezronite, and we had two sons. We left here because of the famine and went to live in Moab. My husband died, and my sons married. During a storm my sons died, so I have come back to the city of my birth. Today I found my father's field markers, as he left them. I claim my father's land as my lawful inheritance." Naomi took a breath.

The elders nodded and one spoke. "We have heard of your return, daughter of Jashuv, and we know of your inheritance. We will honor your right to it. But the land has been used as a public field all these years; men without land of their own have sown and reaped it many times. Although you have returned at harvest time, you are not entitled to any of the yield on it. After this season's grain has been gathered, you may build a home and live on your farm."

"Unfortunately, I don't have the means to build a home, or sow grain on my land."

The elder shook his head. "It's not enough just to claim land; it's too valuable to lie idle. Have you no one to plow and seed it? No one to inherit it?"

"Yes, Honored Councilor, I have. Even though of all my family only I am left, I have my son's wife by my side. She is my daughter Ruth, a Hezronite by marriage."

The elders subjected Ruth to a searching appraisal. Naomi gave her a sidelong glance and felt reassured. The long dress and coat of blue-dyed wool was unadorned, yet rich in its soft texture and fullness. A filmy blue veil enhanced the delicacy of Ruth's features and the pale gold of her hair. There was no servility in her posture; she stood gracefully erect, her manner serene.

At long last the elder spoke. "State the place of her birth."

Loudly and distinctly Naomi said, "Moab . . ."

She felt the hundreds of eyes boring even deeper into her back.

"I beg the council to hear me out." In well-chosen words Naomi sketched Ruth's character. She left out nothing, recounting every incident proving Ruth's love and loyalty to Naomi's God. She concluded that whatever belonged to her was Ruth's also, by right of kinship.

The marketplace was hushed. Everyone, elders and audience, listened in stupefaction as the daring Judean woman praised her Moabite daughter-in-law in the presence of the highest council and the male populace—and in the middle of waiting, unfinished legal business!

The unusual civility of the listeners had given Naomi confidence. When she was finished talking, she felt sure of Ruth's acceptance.

But the elder said coldly, "We are wondering about the real reasons for your action in regard to the Moabitess."

Naomi was unprepared for what the elder said. She waited.

"Whether you are alive or dead, the Moabitess will never inherit your land. Only a born Hebrew can own it. If you were so concerned about your daughter-in-law's welfare, why did you bring her here? As a wife and mother who fled the famine so long ago, you know that the food supply in Bethlehem is always uncertain. That you encouraged the Moabitess to come here, and be a burden on the community, shows great selfishness on your part."

The roar of approval of the assembly was not as loud in Naomi's ears as the pounding of her heart. She could not distinguish the exact words the men were shouting, but she knew they were ridiculing her and Ruth.

Again she wanted to grasp Ruth's hand and run, but she held herself still, head unbowed. Wave after wave of derisive cries from the audience swept over the two women.

The elder motioned his dismissal of the two women.

But as the noise subsided, Naomi spoke one last time. "I ask the council to notify the townsmen that I wish to sell my land. My daughter-in-law and I will never become public charges."

Humiliated, but with their heads high, Naomi and Ruth made their way past the men, crossed the marketplace to their hut, and barred the door.

After a sleepless night, Ruth rose early and dressed in her own coarse clothes.

"Mother, it's time to seek work."

"My child," Naomi said, "I'm afraid that after our appearance before the elders yesterday no one will hire us. The anger of my kinsmen hasn't yet had time to cool."

"Our money won't go far."

"I know."

"Then I'll go now to glean what I can in the fields."

The older woman's head dropped. Ruth had remembered what Naomi had said about gleaning as the Judean way of giving charity to the poor. They were poor, she had to admit. But she dreaded what might happen to her gentle daughter-in-law among the fiercely competitive poor. "Don't . . ." she was about to say.

Ruth read Naomi's true thoughts. "Don't be afraid for me, Mother. I'll glean only in the field of the master who will accept me as a poor woman, no different than the rest."

Ruth fell into step with the people hurrying out the gates. By now her name and Naomi's were on everyone's lips; she could tell by the side glances and whispering around her.

When she came to Naomi's farm and saw the poor already gathered there, she didn't stop but walked far out to the vast field where a steward-in-charge was talking to the waiting crowd of gleaners. Ruth caught his last words. " . . . And you can't go in until the binding girls have rounded the first corner. Then, I will let all of you in at one time. You must be patient until then."

Ruth attached herself to the group. "May I glean here?" she asked the overseer. "I'm a stranger."

The man took no special notice of her. "You're welcome to glean. Boaz, my master, has compassion for all who are in need. Just tell me your name."

"I'm called Ruth."

He knew the name. "Are you the Moabitess who came with Naomi, the Bethlehemite?"

The people made a wide circle away from her.

"Yes."

The overseer hesitated: it was on the tip of his tongue to send her away. He wanted no clashes on his field between Judeans and Moabites. He looked into the young woman's eyes. There was something about her . . . she didn't look like the kind who made trouble. His master would not like it if he found out that a needy person, a stranger, had been turned away. He decided to let the woman glean until the master arrived.

CHAPTER 16

"Father, come with me to the council meeting tonight," said Moshe. They were jogging along the road on white asses, as befitted men of wealth.

"You know I can't abide those meetings," said Boaz. "They bore me."

"Oh no, you would not have been bored last night. It was a meeting to remember."

"Was it?"

"Two women showed up: a widow of Bethlehem and her widowed Moabite daughter-in-law. The Hebrew woman came presumably to claim her father's property. Her name is Naomi and her husband was Elimelek, a Hezronite. Aren't the Hezronites kinsmen belonging to our Perezite clan?"

"Yes," said Boaz, interested. "They belong to the Perezites. Elimelek must have been a clansman of mine."

"Well, this Naomi tried to foist her Moabitess on the council as inheritor to her land. You can imagine how the elders reacted: I thought the blood would come bursting out of their veins.

"What did the widow have to say?"

Moshe recounted all he had heard from Naomi's lips about her daughter-in-law. "The elders let her talk until she was finished, then chopped her down by telling her to keep herself and her daughter-in-law from being nuisances. The elders did it to make them examples to other women who were considering overstepping their places. You would have thought the widow and the Moabitess would have wept and ran away, but not this Naomi. She offered her property for sale!"

Boaz considered this. "Where's the property? If it's any good, I can use it."

"It's small, but I think valuable, close by in Ephrat."

"I'll inquire further about it."

They jogged on in silence for a while. "Moshe, after my harvest is in, I'll be traveling," Boaz said.

"Any special reason?"

"I'm restless. I always used to look forward to working in the fields with my helpers, but it's lost its zest for me. You and your siblings are busy with your families. You no longer need me. I'm thinking that before I'm too old, I'd like to see other places."

"Too old? Father, there's still a spring in your walk. I don't want to hear of your getting old!"

"Moshe, your words lift me up, but—"

"Father, listen to me. My brothers and I have discussed this matter: we're aware that you aren't happy, that you're lonely. Please don't think us forward, but we're of the opinion that you should marry."

Boaz hesitated. "I have given it thought, but I was afraid my sons would resent a new wife whose children would share in their inheritance."

"Is that why you have avoided marriage?"

"No, to be honest, I'm disgusted by the widows who constantly throw themselves at me. I loathe their mannerisms. Their husbands have left them wealthy and they squeeze the life's blood from their servants by overworking and underfeeding them. They shave their heads and wear wigs like the upper-class gentile women. They copy the customs and religion of the Canaanites by filling their houses with nude statues. No, I'm not interested in marrying if it involves these widows. True, I'm lonely, but I want a different kind of woman, one of understanding."

Moshe nodded. "I hope you find such a woman," he said.

"Thank you my son." Boaz smiled at Moshe.

The steward was waving to them from across the field. Boaz began to ride in his direction.

"Wait" said Moshe. "Will you come to me tomorrow? I need your advice on the construction of my east barn."

Boaz nodded and waved goodbye to his son. He passed three of his reapers and greeted them: "May God bless you."

They stopped their work to answer: "And may His blessings be on you."

As he rode along, Boaz saw the day's gleaners scurrying, stooping, pushing to be first to gather what fell from the hands of the harvesters. A lone woman gleaned behind the others on land that had already been picked over.

Even before he asked his steward, "Who is that woman?" he had an idea who she was.

"Master, the Moabite widow came early and has worked without rest. She has caused no trouble. Did I do right to let her stay?"

"Of course," said Boaz, "but where she gleans now, she'll never achieve a full measure of barley. I'll give her the right to glean ahead of the others. Go and tell the menservants not to hinder the foreign woman."

The steward ran to carry out the order as Boaz rode up to the stranger. When he addressed her, Ruth rose respectfully, and Boaz was impressed by her demeanor: she stood erect, her eyes unafraid. He thought, *She'll be set upon if she goes elsewhere.*

"Peace be with you. I am Boaz, the owner of this field."

"Peace be with you, Master."

"Listen to me," he said. "Glean in no other field but this one. Watch where my maidservants bind the sheaves and follow them closely. There you'll find your gleanings more rewarding. Don't fear my men: I'll forbid them to harm you. Whenever you are thirsty, take a drink from their water jars."

Ruth was so surprised by this unexpected generosity that the bewilderment showed in her eyes. Bowing low, she asked, "Why have I found favor with you, that you should take notice of me, seeing that I am a foreigner?"

He answered simply, "I've been informed of all that you have done for your mother-in-law. Your reward will surely come from God, under whose wings you have taken shelter."

Then the steward called out that it was time for the midday meal. Boaz smiled. "Come with me. You will share our meal and dip your bread in our grape-vinegar."

At a discreet distance, Ruth followed Boaz to the place where the hungry harvesters were already seated in a congenial circle. Ruth sat with the girls, opposite Boaz and the men. With his eyes on her, Boaz acknowledged Ruth to be a believer in God like the rest of the circle when he blessed the food and drink in the name of the Eternal One.

"Here," he motioned, as he pushed bread and parched corn in a huge bowl across the ground for Ruth. "Eat heartily."

Boaz's actions were not lost on the other men and women, and Ruth was embarrassed. She wanted to draw away because she was disturbed by the actions of this unusual man. But he was insistent, so she took bread and a handful of the corn, and the cupful of wine he pressed on her. She thought: *He's defying the entire city of Bethlehem by treating me in this way. Why is he doing it? Whatever his reasons . . . he's the first man I've met since Mahlon died that I don't fear.* When everyone took a second helping of the parched corn, Ruth slipped hers into her belt to save for Naomi.

The rest of the day, when the other gleaners scrambled over the wide field, Ruth stayed close behind the women. Boaz sent word to the harvesters that they were to allow the widow to glean even among the bound sheaves. "Pull out some stalks from the bundles and drop them for her to glean. Look away when she picks them up, so she won't know you've done it on purpose."

That night Boaz slept soundly. He had put in a hard, satisfying day of work . . . and the widow Ruth had filled her shawl until it was heavy with gleanings.

He rose early the next morning, eager to return to the harvesting, when he remembered that he had promised Moshe his help. For the next two days he was involved in the building of his son's barn. On the third day when he approached his own field, his eyes immediately searched for Ruth. Why did he feel such a warmth when he saw her there?

He worked every day afterward, looking forward to the noon-time meal and enjoying the jovial banter with the field hands while Ruth watched him, silent but smiling.

The weeks flew by and the day came when all his barley and wheat fields lay bare. Only he and the steward were left to watch as an oxcart drew away the last of the sheaves to the threshing floor.

The servant asked, "Master, will you come early to start the threshing tomorrow?"

Boaz nodded, his eyes on the fields, empty of grain and Ruth.

Why am I not as happy as before? he wondered. *Why am I not anticipating the threshing tomorrow?*

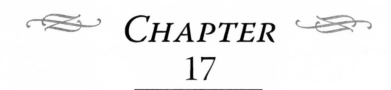

CHAPTER 17

On the morning when Ruth set out to search for a place to glean, Naomi had waited in the hut until the early morning workers were gone from the marketplace.

I'm in no frame of mind to hear the insults of my fellow Judeans, she thought bitterly. *But, I must speak to someone. I'll talk with the Eternal One in His high place.*

The high place was the level top of a graded hill adjacent to Bethlehem. Three religious objects were there: a stone table that was an altar, a large upright stone, and a wind-bent tree. It was God's unenclosed sanctuary.

Naomi took off her shoes before stepping on the hallowed platform. She sat down by the tree and felt the soft wind caress her hair and face.

Eternal One, help me, for I've made a laughing stock of Ruth and myself. I was wrong to force the attention of the council on us, but how else could I have made Ruth known?

Why is there such a burning desire in me to live nobly? Why can't I humble myself to beg as other widows do? Why do I hesitate to use my widowhood and Ruth's to seek shelter and food from relatives?

You've given me the mind and will to live; You've given me the eyes to find the righteous path, so why can't I see a way to save Ruth and myself from beggary?

Where did I go wrong? Through legal ways I appealed to men, and was judged by men, and condemned by men. Can it be that was the mistake? Should I have found a solution in a woman's way? Is there such a way? Is there ... ?

She lifted her face to the warm sun in the blue, cloudless sky. Unaccountably, her spirits soared. She had talked to the Eternal One and though she had no answer, she had peace in her heart. She decided to return home and wait for Ruth. She didn't want her daughter-in-law to find her gone, should she come back early after a fruitless morning's search for a place to glean.

The morning stretched into afternoon. The sun's shadows lengthened into dusk and still Ruth didn't come. Naomi was filled with dread. *What if she is lying hurt and beaten by the Judeans who resent her presence? I have to find her and save her! Which direction should I run to? No . . . I can't run wildly through the countryside. I have to wait here.*

When finally she saw the young woman coming through the gates, her relief was so great that she didn't trust herself to speak without crying like a child. With a smile, Ruth came into the hut and delightedly dropped her bulging shawl at Naomi's feet. Naomi drew Ruth close to her, and the love that flowed between them was wordless.

"Mother, open the shawl."

Naomi knelt on the floor, opened the shawl, and scooped up handfuls of the gray-gold grain. Almost a half-ephah of barley lay there.

"And here is more!" Ruth handed Naomi the roasted ears saved from the noon meal. They divided the corn and ate in silent enjoyment: it was Naomi's first meal since the one Kezia had given them the day before.

Her anxiety and hunger appeased, Naomi asked, "Where did you glean today? A blessing on the owner. Who is he?"

"The owner's name is Boaz."

"Boaz . . . Boaz?" Surprise lighted Naomi's face. "Ruth, this is the man we heard about, a kinsman to Father Natan."

"Yes, he is the one. He told me to keep close to his reapers until they had finished all the harvesting, both of barley and of wheat."

"Oh, Ruth, how good of him! First thing tomorrow, I will take some grain to the baker in exchange for bread, and I'll do likewise with the milk vendor and the oil merchant."

The next weeks were bountiful ones for Ruth, but they left Naomi puzzled. *How does Ruth manage to gather a full shawl of grain from just a day's gleaning? I'm uneasy, but I don't know why, since Ruth seems so content in her work.*

The barley harvest was over and the gleaners followed the harvesters to the wheat fields. At last, one day Naomi had to say, "My child, I'm overwhelmed by the large amount of wheat you've gleaned each day. Who gives us the extra portion of grain?"

The young woman blushed. "Mother, our kinsman Boaz is our bene-factor. I didn't know it, but when I first came he told his harvesters to drop more corn where I was gleaning. Later, I discovered that whenever Boaz walked by me and saw that there was little in my shawl, word would reach the reapers and I would find much grain lying in my path. I dare not tell him in the presence of the other gleaners that I know of his thoughtful-ness. I wish I could thank him, but there's no occasion to see him alone."

Naomi noted Ruth's blush. *Thank You, Eternal One for the way You are pointing out to me.*

Naomi went to Kezia for information about Boaz. That he was rich, eligible for marriage, and influential was obvious. "Kezia, I want to know about his character, the things about Boaz that are below the surface."

Her good friend teased, "Naomi, if I were younger and a widow, I would try to win him for my husband. But, Boaz is a wary man and much too clever to be ensnared by designing females. He treats his children with love and consideration. He has never backed away from a fight, but he doesn't seek trouble. He is generous, but he will not allow any man to steal from him. He is wise and independent enough to act according to his own beliefs, no matter on whose toes he treads. He is a Judean of the highest ideals. Naomi! Are you casting your net for him?"

"Kezia! I'm curious about him because he has been so kind to Ruth, especially after the public rebuke she and I received. He has even let her gather corn unmolested in his fields."

"Knowing Boaz as I do, I would say he was favoring Ruth because he so often disagrees with the thinking of Bethlehem's elders."

"Oh."

The seven weeks of harvesting were almost over. The wheat, like the bar-ley, had been cut and bound into sheaves, then taken away in carts to the threshing floor. Soon there would be nothing left in the fields to glean. The time of Ruth's association with Boaz was nearing its end.

Naomi thought about it day and night. *If only Boaz could see Ruth when she is looking her prettiest, in Kezia's clothes, bathed and scented with perfumed oils, her hair washed and combed until it shines. But, where can Boaz see her other than in the fields? Where can she talk to him freely?*

Another thought intruded itself.

What will Ruth and I do when the gleaning is over and our savings are gone? I'll have no choice but to beg for home and food. I don't want to abase myself to Zerah's unhappy household. I would rather kneel to Boaz, claim my kinship, distant as it is, and pray that he grants us his protection. No matter what he gives us, positions as maidservants or bonded slaves, Ruth and I would have shelter.

That easy solution was soon dispelled. *No, I can't go to Boaz's house. What if he refuses us? We'll be reviled wherever we go. Ruth and I will end up hiding from everyone and starving to death.*

She put her head in her hands, despairingly. Suddenly a bold thought struck her. *Ruth! It's only Ruth who can ask him, and her appeal must take place on the night he's away from home, when he is living on the threshing floor.*

Naomi realized the risk Ruth would be taking if she acted on Naomi's idea. The law said that Hebrew men must not defile themselves with foreign women because they might bring their idols into Judah. Boaz might resent Ruth's petition and expose her, loudly accusing her of accosting him in the night.

We have everything to lose, Naomi told herself. *Me, the Hebrew mother directing the foreign-born daughter . . . my honored name, my burial place beside my father, my inheritance, my trusted word not to bring shame to the community. Everything! And the final price we would pay for our brazenness—death by stoning in the marketplace!*

Naomi shuddered. She had to make a choice. Life was sweet in spite of its hardships and injustices: it was a joy to feel the sun and wind on her face. It was blissful to warm her feet in the newly turned earth, to touch the soft fleece of a newborn lamb. It was good to eat the fruit and the honey, to drink the milk and the wine of her birthplace. But to live a good life in humiliation because she needed the charity of others? She decided to chance her life that Ruth would succeed, and that they both would live worthily.

Naomi's day of action came the morning Ruth returned home early, her shawl empty of gleanings.

Casually, Naomi asked, "Have you heard whether Boaz goes to the threshing floor to guard the grain?"

"Yes, Mother. I've heard the field servants say that he works with them during the days and doesn't leave the threshing floor at night."

"Then please, my daughter, answer my question without reservation. Has Boaz shown himself to be a true kinsman to us?"

There was a perplexed look in Ruth's eyes. "Yes."

"My ambition," Naomi confided, "is to see you settled in his home as his wife. But we have no social standing, no men to arrange a marriage for you. I have thought of every way possible to have Boaz see you as you really are: beautiful, loyal, understanding. Will you listen to my plan?"

Ruth nodded. "Mother, I will do as you say."

"I have called on Kezia for her finest dress and warmest mantle. She gave me ointments and perfumes. Bathe and anoint yourself, then dress in Kezia's clothes. When it grows dark, go near the threshing floor, but do not disclose yourself: wait until all have gone to sleep. Mark well the place where Boaz lies down.

"You'll see that the threshers cover themselves snugly against the cold of the night. When he is asleep, lie down near Boaz and remove the blanket from his feet. If and when he awakens, make yourself known to him. He'll tell you what to do."

"Mother, I have followed your ways and found them righteous for me. Help me prepare myself."

Threshing time was the occasion for great social activity as well as work. Every farmer, his family, and servants joined in the fun. The threshing floor was a table-like area that served as Bethlehem's community-owned commons. The floor itself was a huge, circular, well-drained high plateau of earth, stamped flat and hard with years of usage. Located on an open rise of ground, the threshing floor caught the sweep of strong, widespread winds.

Although the nights were cold, the days were hot and sunny and threshing was thirsty work. Everyone drank the refreshing wine-vinegar and worked with gusto and laughter. At night when the families went home, the unmarried men and girls remained to guard the community's grain. Those were the best times of all: they ate their evening meal before a huge bonfire, told stories, danced, and sang.

The girls vied for the chance to dance with Boaz. "Come, Master, join our circle and hold our hands," they begged. Boaz joined the circle, and they whirled to the lively music of pipe, harp, and drum, until breathlessly they all had to stop. At last in the late hour the boys and girls grew weary. One by one, they picked up a blanket and found a sheltered sleeping place against the sheaves until only Boaz remained.

Alone, all merriment gone, he sat gazing somberly at the fire. *Why am I not enjoying myself? The harvest is successful: there will be plenty of food for everyone in Bethlehem this year. My sons and I will profit from our yield.*

Late into the night Boaz sat, staring into the dying flames. He saw pictures of his lonely life, knowing full well that even travel would not fill the void. The fire was almost out when he realized he had been sitting there a long time.

Sighing deeply, he rose, banked the ashes, picked up a blanket, and chose a sleeping place away from all the others. The wind was gusting, and since his short farmer's tunic reached only to his knees, he covered his feet and legs first, tucking in the lower portion of the blanket securely under him. Then drawing the rest of it up over his shoulders, he fell into a restless sleep.

In his dreams, Boaz's loneliness was like a cold mist enveloping him. He was wandering through the grayness without purpose, and in his straying, he became colder and colder, so cold that at last it awakened him.

The bottom of the blanket covering his feet was not there, and his bare legs were numb with cold. Irritated that the blanket had blown off, he half-rose on one elbow and felt in the dark for the missing cover. His hand touched something trembling and warm. Instantly alert to danger, he gripped the living thing, viselike, as he snatched the knife from his belt.

There was a muffled cry of pain.

"Who are you?"

"I'm Ruth, your field servant."

He pulled her up close to him to see her face. The hood of the cloak fell away. It was Ruth.

This woman had been so often in his thoughts that, after the first shock of touching her arm, Boaz didn't feel any surprise. His heart beat wildly. It was as if he had willed her to be at his side, and she was.

"I am Ruth, your handmaiden," she repeated nervously. "I've come to you because you're my kinsman."

How different she looked! The starlight illuminated her lovely face and eyes; her hair, brushing his face, was smoothed with intoxicating perfume; he could feel the luxurious texture of her dress and the softness of her body. Boaz wanted to laugh aloud from sheer happiness. Had she known from their first meeting that he loved her? He had told her so in everything he did for her.

His arms tightened around her as he kissed her gently. With his lips against her hair he said softly, "Bless you for showing this interest in me at the end of our association in the fields, rather than at the beginning when I might have suspected your interest. I'm happy that you've chosen me, instead of a younger man."

Ruth looked into his eyes.

"Listen to me," he said. "I desire you above all women but I will not take advantage of you. I'm your kinsman and if I take you as a Hezronite widow to marry, I must follow the law that says the closest kinsman to your husband has the first bid to marry you. In that way he acquires whatever valuable property is yours. There is an uncle, older than I, who is closer kinsman to you. I must talk with him to gain my own purpose in marrying you."

The cold wind swept across the threshing floor, riffling Ruth's hair. Tenderly Boaz drew the hood over her head and shoulders. Enfolding her, he whispered, "Stay with me for a while. The first thing in the morning I will find Uncle Zerah and tell him about you. If he wishes to marry you, you'll have to accept him. But I'll ask him in such a way that he'll refuse. Then I promise you, as surely as the Eternal guides us, I'll do the kinsman's part in marrying you."

As he talked, Boaz could feel the compliant weight of Ruth's body against him: she was succumbing to the warmth and security of his arms. With her eyes closed, she rested her head on his shoulder. She had had a night full of uncertainty, from which she was now released.

"Lie down, my love," he said. "I'll keep watch over you. Before the day breaks I'll awaken you."

And while Ruth slept, Boaz dreamed of a happy marriage again: when his welfare, his going and his coming, would be important to the person he loved.

He smiled to himself. He knew it was her mother-in-law who had told Ruth what to do. Naomi would be the matriarch of his household and, if she looked out for his interests as daringly as she did for Ruth's, he would be so much the richer!

He had to thank Naomi for another facet to this marriage. Without Naomi, he would not be able to take Ruth for a wife because of her Moabite birth and her children could not inherit equally to his other children. Naomi gave Ruth Judean family status.

The black of the night lost its intensity; the stars were fading. Reluctantly Boaz awakened Ruth.

"I don't want to disturb your sleep, dear one, but you must be gone before you can be recognized."

Fully awake, happy beyond measure, Ruth pressed Boaz's hand to her lips.

Then Boaz said, "Wait! Take off your scarf, hold it as a sack."

Noiselessly, he moved to a grain pit and with his hands shoveled the cleaned cereal into the scarf. When it was filled, he embraced Ruth quickly and watched as she disappeared into the early morning.

The gates were open when Ruth returned to find her mother-in-law sitting by the door. Naomi had already made up her mind.

If Ruth fails, I will put this bundle of her belongings into her hand and force her to leave Bethlehem at once. No matter how much she objects, she has to leave me and go to safety. I'm Judean: I can face the consequences of my act.

Anxiously she greeted Ruth. "Who are you, wife or widow?"

"Oh, Mother, I will be his wife!"

Naomi hugged her daughter-in-law. "Oh, my child, I must give thanks to the Eternal One. I must go to His high place. Rest now and wait. The sort of man Boaz is, he won't waste time waiting for things to happen. He'll make them happen. We'll have word from him today!"

She ran off, leaving Ruth to watch alone.

Boaz waited on the threshing floor for his steward to awaken. "I'm going to the gates and won't return today," he said.

He mounted his white donkey and rode off. When he arrived in the marketplace, he tied the donkey to a stone post. He found a seat on the ground close to the gates and waited for his uncle Zerah to walk out. "Ho! My uncle!" he called when he saw the old man. "It's Boaz. Peace be with you. Come, sit with me."

The old man, stooped with age, looked down with surprise at his busy nephew calmly seated by the gates at the start of a workday morning. What could be the matter?

"Peace be with you, Boaz," he said, as he lowered himself stiffly. "What do you want of me?"

His greeting was lost on Boaz, who at that moment caught sight of a group of elders going out the gates.

"Most respected councilors!" he called loudly. "The Eternal bless your judgments! Come sit with us. We're in need of your services."

The men hesitated. One elder spoke out, "Boaz, we have much to do. Can't you wait until tonight?"

"Tonight is too late. This won't take long."

When they were all seated, Boaz addressed his kinsman. "Uncle, you have no doubt heard that the widow Naomi, daughter of Jashuv, has returned from Moab and is selling her father's land. By marriage it belonged to her husband, Elimelek, who was our close kinsman. If you want the land, then buy it, since yours is the prior right. If you don't want it, then tell me now, for I'm next to redeem it."

Zerah took his time answering. Of course he had heard about the widow Naomi, but he was getting absent-minded and had forgotten that her land was for sale. He looked at Boaz appreciatively. What a good boy Boaz was to remind him about that excellent piece of property.

"I'll buy it!" he said.

"Uncle, I must also remind you that when you buy Naomi's land you are purchasing her daughter-in-law, the woman Ruth from Moab, who is the widow of Elimelek's son. The land is all that Ruth has, and whoever is the redeemer must also be her husband. It's the only righteous way she can marry and beget children to carry on her husband's name."

Zerah listened closely. The council members and Boaz waited.

Slowly, anger spread over the old man's face. He shook a trembling finger. "No! No! You're proposing that at my age I should marry a young widow so that she can bear children for her dead husband? I refuse! It would injure me physically. It would disrupt my household! My old wife would never give me peace! As for my children, there would be strife over their inheritance if it's threatened by a Moabitess's children. No! No! As far as I am concerned you can have the widow's land. I give you my claim to it."

Zerah was so perturbed over the whole affair that he was struggling to get up to get away, but Boaz held him down. "Wait, Uncle, there's one more thing you must do. Since you are rejecting your kinsman's land and widow, you must make it legal and binding."

"What? Now what are you up to?"

"Let the council answer for me."

The elders, who had listened restlessly to the two men talk about their affairs while their own duties were pressing, were plainly annoyed.

"Boaz! Out of respect for you we delayed our work. Now you want us to make legal judgments in a hurry? We are not prepared to hold council at this moment. Since it concerns the Moabitess, we have to get other opinions. Again we ask you, wait until tonight."

"No, I can't wait. Time is valuable to me, too. The question of the widow's birthplace is not as important as the fact that I would make this woman my wife today. You've already heard my uncle's decision. Only tell us the law."

"You wish to marry the foreigner? The Moabitess?" The elders didn't dare to voice their disapproval. Boaz wasn't a man to take unasked for opinions. Drawing aside, they consulted in low tones, and when they returned to the uncle and nephew, the spokesman said, "Zerah, your nephew has challenged us to dredge our minds for old laws. This particular law is little known because it's seldom that an incident such as this one arises. But, the law is this: Because no money is paid or a contract written up, to show the assembly and council that you relinquish all claims to the widow and her land, you must loose the shoe from your foot and hand it to Boaz."

Scowling, Zerah bent over and with shaking fingers untied his shoe. As he handed it to Boaz, he said shortly, "You are free to claim our kinsman's inheritance."

Boaz rose and held the shoe aloft. He addressed the council and the growing crowd of interested onlookers. "All of you are witnesses that today I intend to buy land that belonged to my dead kinsmen Elimelek and Mahlon, through their widows Naomi and Ruth. Also, I will marry Mahlon's widow, the Moabitess. If we have children, they'll bear the name of Mahlon's family and ensure that it won't be forgotten in this city, where it's held in high esteem."

The listeners admired the man. "You've done a righteous deed," said one man. "I'm proud to be your witness."

Another said, "May you find the woman you have chosen to be fruitful in bearing children like our ancestresses Rachel and Leah, whose children built the House of Israel."

Boaz waved his thanks to all of the men, then knelt down to tie the shoe back on Zerah's foot before he helped the old man up. The need for an audience was over. Everyone dispersed.

With a dignified pace, Boaz walked across the marketplace to Naomi's hut, which he knew by the crowd gathered before it. He knocked on the door. Instantly Ruth opened it. Boaz stooped to enter the low doorway, then closed the door against the curiosity of those watching.

Ruth was still in Boaz's arms when Naomi returned. Boaz saw a tall, thin woman whose eyes were so spirited and intelligent that he immediately liked what he saw. Naomi saw a poised, black-haired man of middle years who, in his short farmer's tunic, looked young and vigorous. Un-self-consciously, he kissed Ruth once again, and said to Naomi, "Mother, with your blessings and the council's knowledge, I take Ruth in marriage this very day. Come, let us leave this gloomy place."

Shouldering the shawl of grain he had given Ruth, he walked out. Hastily, the women gathered their few possessions and hurried after him.

When they entered Boaz's house, mother and daughter were awed by the splendor. The house had been built to accommodate Boaz's large family; now it was empty of everyone except Boaz and the servants.

No wonder he was ripe for marriage again, thought Naomi. *Such a great house, bereft of wife and children, would deepen a man's loneliness.*

Naomi wandered alone through it, while Boaz, as excited as a boy, showed Ruth all of his treasures. Naomi found the room for the women servants and dropped her little bundle in a corner, grateful that she would have a place.

"Mother!" called Boaz impatiently. He and Ruth found Naomi in the servants' room.

"Mother, I have many things to do," Boaz told Naomi. "Would you help me by preparing my bride and our wedding feast?"

Naomi smiled and said yes.

"Whatever you need is at your command: the food, the clothes, the servants, the house. Do as you see fit. I must go to my sons and daughters and invite them and their families to the wedding festivities, which we'll hold this night."

And before the women could say anything, he was out in the yard instructing a manservant to fetch the white ass he had left in the marketplace, while he threw a saddle blanket over another one and spurred the animal to a fast trot.

Naomi and Ruth looked at each other in bewilderment. They were relieved when a servant came into the room. He smiled at Ruth, but bowed to Naomi. "The master instructed me to show you the storehouse. When you have decided on the food to be readied for tonight, I will carry out your orders."

"Mother!" Ruth whispered. "This is surely Boaz's way of saying he entrusts you to run his household. He has made you a matriarch."

Naomi's eyes were shining. "I'm overwhelmed," she said. "But come, we have no time to waste talking."

Shortly after Ruth and Boaz were married, Ruth became pregnant. She and Boaz and Naomi awaited the birth with eager expectation, but at the end of nine months the child hadn't come, and Ruth suffered prolonged spasms of pain.

Naomi grew more and more worried. *Ruth is no longer young or robust. Lack of food and hard labor in Moab and gleaning for long hours in Bethlehem have weakened her. She may not have the strength to live through these repeated attacks.*

Ruth saw the concern in Naomi's eyes. "Mother, please don't watch me so closely. I feel fine. Please go outdoors for a breath of air. I will call you the moment I need you. Boaz is working close by, too."

"Perhaps you're right. I will go out, for just a little while to the Eternal's High Place. I won't be long."

Naomi hurried up the hill to the peaceful sanctuary. She slipped off her shoes and knelt under the sacred tree to beg the Eternal for His help. Then she ran home. Ruth might be needing her at this very moment.

It was Kezia who opened the door. She had brought Leah and Shulamit. "We came to see if your grandchild is here yet. When Ruth greeted us at the door, we knew we were too soon, but she insisted we wait for you."

Naomi was glad for the company; it would help Ruth while away the time if she could listen to the women's gay chatter. But they were no sooner seated when Ruth's face twisted into a grimace of pain.

"Wait here." Naomi said to her friends as she helped Ruth into the bedchamber.

As the agonizing pains came more frequently, Naomi saw that Ruth's lips were bleeding; she was trying to hold back her screams.

Naomi heard herself using the very words Mother Malkah had spoken at Mahlon's birth: "My daughter, cry out against the evil spirits!"

Ruth gave birth to a son that hour. The struggle to bring the child out exhausted both mother and midwife, but Naomi slapped life into the baby, and after cleansing and swaddling the infant, cleansed and cared for the mother. When finally she opened the door, the women rushed past her to see the infant in his cradle.

Naomi found Boaz. "You have a son!"

Boaz couldn't speak because of his joy. Like a new father, he hugged Naomi, then bounded off to see the baby and Ruth.

Naomi was more weary than she could ever remember. She dropped into a chair, her hands resting limply in her lap. Yet her heart was light. Ruth was alive and so was the baby.

Out of the bedchamber came the women, the bundled baby in Kezia's arms. She laid the child in his grandmother's lap. "Naomi, you are indeed a fortunate woman! Not only do you have the child to raise, but you also have Ruth, who loves you dearly. She has been of greater worth than seven sons. Boaz wants you to name the child."

Naomi's eyes filled with tears. "Little one," she said to her grandson, "what name shall I choose for you?"

The women all had suggestions, but none of the names pleased Naomi. She shook her head.

"I have just thought of a wonderful name," said Kezia. "Oved!"

"Oved?" repeated Naomi. "Oved . . . Oved . . ." Naomi examined each facet of the name. It meant to be of service, to serve as a source of pride. Perhaps Oved would someday serve as a learned elder in the council? Then she thought, *No, Oved can serve in even greater capacity. With his inheritance of mind and strength, love and loyalty, he can be a hero-leader to his people. He can rise up and save us from the onslaughts of rabble Canaanites. And why should he save only us? The Philistines are at this moment crushing the clans of Reuven, even now enslaving our fellow Judeans. Eventually, it must be as Father Natan foretold, that Judah will have a king. And the king's name could be . . . Oved. Yes! Oved could serve as Judah's first king!*

The baby's loud cry brought Naomi out of her reverie and back to her friends.

"Oh, my little one, my beautiful Oved, don't cry," she whispered. "I have seen visions of you as a man among men, a king above elders and leaders. Yours is a glorious future. You are the tree whose branches will hold aloft great kings."

"Mother, Ruth heard the baby cry. I will take him to her." Boaz lifted his son gently from Naomi's arms.

Willingly, she gave him up, but did not follow her friends or Boaz into Ruth's room.

Instead, she left them and went outside to climb the stairs to the rooftop. The crisp air, blowing over Judah's hills, cleared Naomi's mind of her dreams.

How good life was in the living of it! How glad she was that she had refused to succumb to the blows life had dealt her! In a world where men ruled, she had used her resoluteness to achieve an honorable place in society. She had won on her own terms.

She breathed deeply; her heart was at peace. Soon the winter would be over and spring would come; life would burgeon again throughout the land. It was spring when she and Ruth returned to Bethlehem, and she recalled the cry torn from her heart as she stood at the well with Kezia: "Call me not Naomi, the name of pleasantness. Call me Marah, for God has dealt bitterly with me." How wrong she had been to say that. Some day soon she would remind Kezia of that cry and she would correct it. She would say, "Life is bitter, yet sweet. It is worth the difficult choices we have to make, the burdens we have to assume, the effort we have to put forth, to have the sweetness overcome the bitterness."

She heard Boaz call up from the yard below, "Mother, we need you."

"Boaz," she answered, "I've just discovered something!"

"Yes?"

"It will be a short winter. Already I can smell the perfume of spring in the air."

And the perfume filled Naomi's heart with song.